ERINGUILD

By

Annie Muscutt

For my Auntie Rosalind, remembered with great love.

CONTENTS

ACKNOWLEDGMENTS

To all who have supported me in this venture, my grateful thanks.

1

The Secret Room

Jeremy Applegate was not looking for an adventure that particular Sunday morning – but then, you rarely are when you find one. Moving with all the excitement boredom would allow, he ambled round the house, rather aimlessly searching for something to do. This had become his routine as his mother, mistaking his sensitive nature for illness, thought it best he remained in the house for the time being at least. Being only seven years old and with a watchful eye upon him, Jeremy was very rarely alone.

The one place he could be was an old room that used to be his father's study. It demanded secrecy, Mother didn't like talking about anything to do with Daddy if she could help it and Jeremy, knowing this, rarely brought him up. The room was excellent for his purpose; as you entered, the slight smell of must filled your nostrils. A beautiful bay window looked out upon the garden and a large oak desk lay in front of that. Jeremy knew all this, despite the room now being covered with white sheets. He had once explored underneath the looming shapes and had raised Mother's temper as well as a cloud of dust, so now contented himself with his memory. He remembered once tracing his finger round a circle of wax, where it had dropped so long ago. This made Jeremy think of his father, picturing him as he sat, hunched over the desk, scrawling frantically against the light of a fading candle. He would stand patiently in the doorway and watch until Daddy's head would look up and his bright smile welcomed him into the room. He would sit in his lap whilst he told wonderful stories, of dragons and witches, in worlds that seemed so real as they came alive in Jeremy's mind.

'Not real,' his mother had said to his father on one occasion. 'Why must you frighten him with these fantasy creatures? Is there not enough real worry in the world for him already?'

Jeremy sighed and thought now of Mother. There was nothing really secret about this room beyond her not knowing the true amount of time he spent in it and yet... He sensed something there. It was somewhere he felt happy and close to his father.

Jeremy sighed again, he thought about his father often but without really having any idea what had happened that day. There had been an argument. He remembered that. Raised voices had brought him from his bed and to the staircase where he clutched the wooden bars and rested his small head against the bannister. And this is what he had heard:

2

Jeremy had recognised the agitated, high voice of his mother.

'It's stupid, Henry. Why do you insist on filling your head with this nonsense? Why can't you just be here for us?'

His father sighed in his patient way. 'Margaret, you just don't understand…'

'No, I don't,' she retorted, 'and neither do I want to. What I want is for you to throw that thing away, burn it, bury it, I don't care but I'm not having it in the house anymore.' She began to cry. 'It's taking you away from us.'

The two shadows Jeremy had been watching so intently had then moulded into one as his mother continued to sob. Jeremy then crept back to his room, pulling up the covers around his face and watching the shadows as they danced on the ceiling. What did Mummy mean and how was Daddy filling his head? Did it open somehow?

Jeremy had slipped into a semi-dreamlike state as he replayed this action in his mind, and was awoken only by the sound of Mother calling him for supper. He checked the room, making sure there was no evidence of his being there, and then quietly slipped out the door. *Everybody has secrets,* he thought as he descended the stairs, little realising how right he was. If truth were told, this house was full of secrets, hovering silently in the air, like whispers never spoken. But this was about to change, as Jeremy Applegate wanted some answers and knew exactly the person who could help him.

2

Questions and Answers

Grandma Finlay sat on the sofa opposite Jeremy, peering over her thin spectacles and appearing to smile without using her mouth. She was a kind-faced old lady with snowy white hair neatly held in a bun, and was as fond of Jeremy as he was of her. He must have been staring intently at her because Grandma suddenly asked: 'What is it, my pet? Do you have a question?'

I have many, thought Jeremy, but decided he would begin in a simple way. 'Granny, can you tell me about Daddy?'

A slight look of pain crossed her face but in a second it was gone.

'Well,' she faltered, leaning back into the sofa and peering towards the kitchen, 'it may not be appropriate.'

'What does that mean?' he asked.

'It means that perhaps you should take me to see that lovely swing of yours,' she replied.

Jeremy didn't see what that had to do with anything, but then he thought adults often did strange things, so he took her hand and led her out into the garden towards the swing. It had been built by his father and had seen better days. The seat was now cracked due to the wind and rain and the ropes were beginning to fray, but Jeremy loved it all the same. 'A fine swing,' Grandma said. 'Would you like a push?' Jeremy nodded and lifted himself into the seat and she began the motion. 'Do you know,' she continued, 'I used to do this for your daddy, just like I am with you. "Higher, Mummy!" he used to say. "As high as you can."' She sighed. 'Always had his head in the clouds, that one.'

And then she suddenly stopped pushing, as if lost in her thoughts.

'You never know what's going to happen in life, Jeremy. That's what makes it an adventure. Here one minute and gone the next, who would have thought it?' she murmured, speaking now more to herself than to him.

'Do you mean Daddy?' he inquired, and she nodded.

'But I can't believe it. It's all so wrong. He never would have left you.' She was now gripping the ropes tightly with both hands, not wanting to let go. 'Lies.' Her voice cracked. 'They were all lies about him. Tarnishing his clever name.' She sniffed.

'I don't understand,' Jeremy said, utterly confused about what she meant.

'Of course you don't, my love, how could you? What I'm saying Jeremy,' and at this point she swirled him round to face her and whispered softly, 'is that your daddy may have gone but I don't think he meant to leave.'

At this point, there was a tap on the French windows and Mother's concerned face was peering out.

'I can't say any more, Jeremy,' Grandma said to him as she waved at Mother. 'I don't want to upset anyone but if you want to be close to your father, look at his books. He loved his books but,' and she hugged him, 'not nearly as much as he loved you. Come on, poppet,' she said cheerfully. 'Let's get some cake.'

She reached out her hand towards him and Jeremy took it. Grandma thought the conversation had finished there as they trudged up the garden, but Jeremy was still thinking about what she had said. Father's books were in the secret room so this wasn't going to be easy. He had to be careful. He felt like a detective searching for hidden clues and if there were any in this house, the secret room was surely where they would be. A sudden tingling sensation ran through his body, as if agreeing with his thoughts.

3

The Secret is Revealed

The following morning Jeremy was awoken by the strong thundering of rain on his window. He pulled back the curtains and peered out. He had not been mistaken. The sky was thick with cloud and only a glimpse of the tree and the swing beneath it could be seen. No hope of going out today. Mother would be relieved. He crossed back over to his bed and sat down, remembering what his grandma had said the previous day about his daddy's books. The secret room was filled with books, some too high to reach and all covered with a thick layer of dust. As it happened, Jeremy was more concerned about reaching them than the difficulty of reading them. He was a strong reader, due to his times of solitude in the house. He was mainly interested in comics and adventure books but he was happy to make an exception.

Mother seemed frustrated this morning as she

clattered round the kitchen. Jeremy sat down to his porridge and looked at his mother. Even at his young age, he knew she had been crying, as the red puffiness stood out on her pretty face. 'You're a good boy,' she said suddenly. 'I know I am very busy and that means that I can't always be with you...' Jeremy cut her off.

'That's all right,' he said quickly, suddenly frantic that his time in the secret room might be already drawing to a close before it had even begun. She smiled a smile that made her look as young as him, and to reassure her, Jeremy planted a kiss on her cheek. 'Thank you for breakfast,' he said. 'May I be excused?' She nodded and he jumped down. Had they been a different sort of family, he would have told her he loved her at that point but although both of them thought it, no further words were spoken as Jeremy left the room.

He walked leisurely up the stairs, knowing that Mother would be unlikely to leave the kitchen during the next hour at least. Jeremy headed for the secret room and once inside, felt again that strange tingle running through his body. He had a steadily growing sensation that there *was* something secret about this room and it was down to him to discover it.

He moved his head slowly upwards, examining the shelves of books one by one. He had the peculiar feeling that he was looking for something but without knowing what. He started to pick books at random, gently blowing the dust from their covers before carefully turning the pages inside. They were nice books but nothing out of the ordinary. Jeremy replaced each one with care, knowing that they belonged to his father.

Suddenly, he looked up in alarm – footsteps were heading this way. Mother! That quick, light step was unmistakable. Jeremy jumped, filled with the panic of being caught. Mother would surely forbid him to go in. She would be hurt with the reminders of Daddy so evident in that room and lock it away out of sight. Jeremy pictured only being able to glimpse the room through the keyhole. He made a dive for the only place he could think to hide – beneath the desk. Under the sheet he went, just as Mother entered the room. Jeremy kept very still and watched her feet. She stopped at the door; he imagined that she was thinking about something and then she took a hesitant step forward. For one awful moment he believed that she was going to reach down and lift the sheet like a terrible game of hide and seek that he didn't want to play. Instead she remained still.

'Jeremy?' she called in a soft and inquiring voice.

Jeremy didn't want to ignore her but knew he couldn't answer either. He sat motionless, crouched under the desk until Mother retreated to the door and closed it behind her. He listened for her footsteps becoming quieter as she walked down the hall until they had disappeared altogether. Jeremy let out a long, slow sigh of relief and prepared to crawl out. As he did so, not judging the height correctly, he banged his head on the underside of the desk. The pain of the blow startled him and he sat down again with a bump. Rubbing his head and looking upwards at the offending furniture, he saw a strange sight. It appeared that with the force of the collision, part of the desk had come loose, displaying what seemed like a hidden drawer. Jeremy crouched up on his knees, taking care not to hurt himself for a second time. What he suspected was quite true, there was a drawer but it hadn't been there before. Jeremy reached inside it and found a small leather-bound notepad. It was tied carelessly with string and had the initials "H.A." Jeremy gasped with the realisation that this belonged to his father, Henry Applegate, but why was he hiding it? He began to untie the string when he heard his mother's voice calling him downstairs.

He scrambled out from under the desk, brushing the dust from his knees. He opened the door with some hesitation, half expecting Mother to be on the other side with her hands firmly placed on her hips, a stern frown covering her face. Fortunately this was not the case and Jeremy, calling back to his mother, walked quickly to his own room. There he concealed the book under his mattress until he was at leisure to inspect it again. As he descended the stairs Jeremy smiled; the secret room did have a secret and now it was his secret too.

*

Over the following days, Jeremy devoted his time to the study of his father's book. This was only interrupted by meals and bedtime and at such times, the book was replaced under his mattress, concealed until the next time he could look at it. Interestingly, the book was full of pictures, sketches of different creatures, most of which Jeremy had never seen before. They reminded him of the people in his father's stories; magical beings brought alive through the imagination. The book seemed to have a strange power over him. The more he looked at it, the more he wanted to do so again. It became harder and harder to put it down and if he was not with it, he was certainly thinking about the next time he could be.

As he dreamt that night, Jeremy stood in a great valley, with mountains towering on either side. A small wind was blowing from behind him and it ruffled his hair. He felt that he was not alone and turned to see a strange being approaching. It was at first in the distance, shadowy to his view, and then, as is possible in dreams, the creature was almost upon him. He beheld a being with both human and animal features. It had a kindly face showing the wisdom of many years, and yet was intimidating by its colossal size. Jeremy, in his dream was unable to move, despite his great urge to run away, and the creature bent down to be near to Jeremy's face, where it paused before it breathed the single word: 'Eringuild.'

Jeremy flinched in his sleep, waking himself up, and he sat up in bed, panting. He looked around, feeling the comfort of his own room. *Thank goodness*, he thought, sinking back and resting his head on his pillow. It had only been a dream.

4

From One World to the Next

Most of us are used to forgetting what happens in our dreams, as the fantasy adventures of our sleep slip away, but Jeremy could not forget. The name Eringuild seemed imprinted in his mind and he was compelled to discover its meaning. First, he tried his father's book, but although the name was repeatedly mentioned in a scribbled way, there was no further explanation. Then he tried looking it up in the dictionary, but again with little success. Jeremy was reluctant to explore the only other option he could think of but the pursuit of knowledge filled him with courage. He walked down to the morning room where as expected, Mother was writing at her desk, holding her pencil with the elegance she applied to most things. Hearing the door open, she looked up and smiled.

'Hello darling.'

The look, although sincere, was only a fleeting glance, as she looked down again at her writing. Jeremy was busy thinking about the best way to ask his question when Mother helpfully started the conversation in the right direction.

'What have you been doing, my love?'

'I'm looking up a new word,' said Jeremy carefully, 'but I can't seem to find it.'

Mother continued to write as she talked but said: 'You are perfectly right to come to me. Developing our minds is extremely important, so perhaps if you tell me the word, we'll look it up together.' Despite this invitation, Jeremy still could not help feeling anxious, but then as if from nowhere that tingle appeared in his body and it somehow spurred him on.

'It's Eringuild,' he spluttered in a rather clumsy way.

Mother dropped her pencil with a clatter and looked up suddenly at her son with a look of complete horror.

'What did you say?' Her question trailed off even as she spoke it.

'Eringuild, Mummy,' said Jeremy, the distress also rising in him, 'I said Eringuild.'

She sprang from the desk and crossed over to him; her face was white and he felt the tremble in her hands when she touched him.

'Where did you hear that word?' she demanded with a tone he had never heard her use before. Jeremy, in the instant of the moment, saw all the things he could not say – the book, the secret room – but was compelled to say something.

'I just thought of it, Mummy, it was there in my head. I was playing a game…'

He began to stumble over the words and Mother softened. She sunk to the floor, pulling Jeremy down to her lap in an unusual display of affection. Pressing his head to her, with one hand on his forehead, as if she were testing his temperature, she said, 'The answer is it isn't a word, Jeremy. It means nothing, it's completely made up, that's how it just appeared in your head and why it's not in any dictionary. You are growing up, my love, and the world is complicated enough. Concentrate on real words; there are enough of them after all. Those are the words that you and I shall talk about and we shall not mention that word again, shall we?'

'No,' said Jeremy. 'I'm sorry, Mummy.'

'Oh, there's nothing to be sorry for,' she said with pretended joviality. 'I just want the best for you, Jeremy. You know that, don't you?'

'Yes Mummy,' said Jeremy as they both got up.

'There's a good boy,' said Mother, returning to her desk. 'See you at lunchtime.'

She turned to the window.

'The sun is coming out, a good day for the swing maybe?'

Jeremy smiled a puzzled smile and closed the door. As he walked down the corridor he heard one short sob from his mother and his face dropped in sympathy. He imagined her head in her hands, bent over the desk, which behind the door was exactly as she was.

Jeremy himself was feeling a great urge to cry. Not only did he feel frustrated and upset but also alone, somehow lost in all that was around him. He ran for the secret room, now without any care whether Mother heard him or not. He suddenly missed his father more than ever and the hot tears of frustration ran down his face. As he ran, questions filtered through his head. Why were things like this? Why was Mother so upset? He began to feel the full force of the loneliness that had been building up inside him over so many months. Trapped inside the house, unable to be a normal little boy. He didn't want it anymore. The secret room was in sight. He ran forward building speed.

'I don't want this anymore!' he shouted. 'I don't want…'

Anyone watching at this point would have seen Jeremy disappear, not into the secret room but into a space between it and the rest of the house. As he had been calling out, something had heard him, something had been listening and it was this thing that had removed Jeremy Applegate from his own world and sent him tumbling into another.

5

Eringuild

For Jeremy, the passage of his journey was over very quickly. One moment he was running through the door of the secret room and the next he was sailing through blackness, falling, falling until…

He landed, surprisingly on his feet, in a place that seemed familiar to him. He was standing on the edge of a precipice, looking out at a land so long, it seemed to go on forever. Either side of him were majestic mountains framing the valley and on the horizon was a patch of land covered in shadow, cold and gloomy without the light. Jeremy looked up and squinted in the bright light. He raised his eyebrows when he witnessed that there were two spheres in the sky, one identical to the sun in our world but the other dark and sinister, as large as the sun and full of deep black craters. At that moment, they appeared to be at opposite ends of the sky and Jeremy felt a strange sort of comfort in that.

A light breeze had begun to blow and Jeremy looked behind him, opening his mouth in awe at what now came towards him. The creature was colossal, as it walked on two legs, with the body shape of a man but with head, hooves, and antlers like a deer. The eyes were huge and brown, gentle and yet somehow fearsome. The creature approached Jeremy and bent down its head as if going to talk. For one moment both stood and looked at each other until the creature said, 'Can you speak?'

Jeremy nodded.

'There is no need to fear, child. I will not harm you. I have been waiting for you here for many months, hoping each day would be the day. And now here you are, Jer-e-my.'

The creature elongated Jeremy's name, as if he was unsure how to say it.

'How do you know my name?' Jeremy asked.

'I know many things about you,' the creature replied. 'I have been calling for you, but not until today did you call back. That is why you are here, I heard your call and here you stand in our land of Eringuild.'

Jeremy gasped, finally realising the meaning of the word.

'Sit child, and listen. I can see your human legs are shaking.'

Jeremy obeyed and plopped himself down on the grass that seemed to bend beneath his weight, moulding to his body. He had never felt so comfortable when sitting. The creature continued: 'Where you stand and all you can see is the land of Eringuild and home of many nations. You come to us in our time of greatest need and it is lucky that you appeared to me and not elsewhere. Others may not have been so welcoming.'

'I don't understand,' Jeremy said. 'How did I get here?'

'We called you, Jeremy, and you answered. Have you not felt the calls? The tingles, the whispers? Who do you think showed you the secret room and who helped you find your father's book?'

'That was you?' Jeremy exclaimed.

'Yes,' replied the creature. 'Many strange things can occur when one world calls to another, but your arrival here has been destined for some time.'

Jeremy was gaining confidence and asked, 'What did you mean, when you referred to the others?'

'Ah,' sighed the creature, 'that requires a further explanation and then you will understand your purpose here. Eringuild is a land made up of many regions, each occupied by a different race. So it has been since the beginning. It is an old story, more like a myth in the present time but this is how it goes.

'A wizard made Eringuild when the land was simply one large place. He was the first inhabitant of Eringuild. As it was already full of many creatures, the wizard crafted a magical golden crown adorned with precious jewels. As all creatures sought to be the ruler of the land, the wizard proclaimed that he who could fit the crown perfectly on his head would rule with his race over all others. All stepped forward to try, even the shadow dwellers from the north. It is said that the wizard blotted out the sun to allow their presence, as they cannot look at the sun. Yet none prevailed. The wizard decided then to melt the crown, fashioning it into a golden acorn set with two rubies. The shape was taken to Tayrah, which is the castle in the very centre of the land, built, as its position is the same distance away from the boundary of all lands. There, an agreement was formed. Each creature would rule in their own part of Eringuild, never leaving unless invited by others, and the acorn would remain as a symbol of peace and shared rule. This was accepted and each returned to their previous home. The giants to the coast, and the shadow dwellers to their dark domain.

'So many years of prosperity and peace prevailed until alas, one day the acorn was stolen from Tayrah! Each race believed the others would seek the acorn and rule for themselves, thinking until the idea consumed them. They became obsessed with finding the acorn for themselves and all others became enemies in their quest. That is why I say you are lucky to have come to me as our time of greatest need walks hand in hand with danger. Eringuild is not the land it was, nothing is as it seems and very few can be trusted. I am one of the Asrahs, one of the last peaceful nations in Eringuild. We are immortal and so have no concern for short-term power. Our mission is to restore peace to Eringuild by finding the acorn, and that is where we need you.'

'But,' said Jeremy, feeling suddenly frightened, 'what can I do? I am just a little boy!'

'Little as you are, you are special, Jeremy. Your father knew about us long ago and tried to tell you through stories. He, too, heard the call, but dabbled too far with its exploration and could not travel back and forth as he once did. He joined us here and is here still.'

'Daddy is here?' said Jeremy.

'Yes,' said the Asrah. 'Where exactly, we are uncertain, but we can work together to find what is important to both of us. What is lost shall again be found.'

6

The Warlock of the Hill

'Where do we start?' questioned Jeremy. 'It seems such a big problem and I'm such a little boy.'

'It is indeed a grave matter,' said the Asrah. 'But we must never forget hope, as small as it may seem.'

'But it's so hard to be hopeful,' said Jeremy, sighing. 'How will we ever find the acorn?'

'These things cannot be told but there is still hope,' his friend replied. 'Most importantly, you are here, which means there's a better chance of finding it than ever before. There would be no hope without you, and you hold the answers to many secrets.'

'How can I?' said Jeremy, feeling confused. 'I only just arrived here.'

'You will know when the time comes, little one,' said the Asrah, patiently. 'But now we begin our quest. The one we must meet with is Tirimae, a wise warlock of the land. He was there at the birth of Eringuild and is one of the few who can help us.'

'How do we find him?' questioned Jeremy.

'He resides in the mountain now, driven away by the destruction that has befallen the land. It is impossible to find the entrance without the setting of the sun. As the sun sinks through the sky this evening, its final resting place will mark the spot.'

He looked up at the sky and sniffed the air.

'It does not leave us with many hours of daylight. We will need to move quickly, there is no time to be lost. Can you do this, Jeremy?'

'I think I can,' Jeremy said, and the Asrah began to move.

'But,' said Jeremy, pausing for a second. 'You know my name but I don't know yours. People travelling together should be introduced, shouldn't they?'

The Asrah turned back towards his small companion and nodded his great head.

'You are wise, Jeremy of the human world,' he said, 'and my name is Gillimal.'

*

They travelled swiftly across the land, Gillimal always watching for passing dangers.

'There are things you must remember,' said the Asrah to Jeremy. 'We are moving through a dangerous land and will be seen as enemies to most others. We must always have our wits about us, Jeremy, as there are those that will throw difficulties in our path. Do not tell anyone of our quest, or in fact tell them anything at all. Trust no one unless I tell you it is safe to do so. Stay by my side so I can protect you, never venture out alone. I am old and wise to the creatures of Eringuild but there are those here that your eyes will have never seen before. Things here will appear like dreams compared to your world but it would be dangerous indeed to think them so.'

It was getting darker now and Jeremy again witnessed the black sun.

'What is that?' he asked Gillimal. He replied without looking, obviously holding some strange power to interpret questions.

'That is the black sun,' Gillimal said. 'It is the symbol of darkness and the shadow that has fallen over our happy land. It appeared the day the acorn was stolen but draws any bad feelings to it, so growing in size and strength. It moves towards our sun and if we do not find the acorn and return it to Tayrah in time, the black sun will conquer and our beautiful land will be cast into shadow forever.'

'That's awful,' said Jeremy, 'and what are the holes in its sides?'

'The black sun is also a home for evil creatures, which grow as it does. The suns here have senses and the black sun is willing us to fail. It will try to obstruct our quest in any way it can and that's why we must move as quickly and quietly as possible.'

The light was now fading fast as they climbed up the mountain. Jeremy had felt a new strength in him since entering Eringuild and walked with a quickness in his step. As they reached the peak of the hill, Gillimal turned and pointed to the sun, which had begun its descent. As it drew closer, the burning light covered the hill, until it had almost disappeared. The last of the light on the mountainside dissolved the grass and displayed a set of shining steps.

'Quickly,' Gillimal said, and the two companions descended inside the hill. As they did, the entrance closed behind them but had they been a moment later, they would have witnessed a crater in the black sun burst and an unknown shape fall silently into the valley below.

*

Gillimal and Jeremy descended into the mountain, twisting and turning as they followed the steps. The remains of the sun's light lingered with them, casting a faint golden glow over the tunnel. Jeremy could make out the roots of trees, whose branches were far away above, rustling in the evening breeze. 'Trees are mainly our friends,' said Gillimal, 'and their roots can be extremely useful. If you know how, they can pass messages between you and the treetop – like a telescope, it can send a message of what it can see back to you. Very helpful if you're ever trapped under the ground.'

Suddenly, as they rounded a corner, the tunnel opened out, displaying a huge underground cavern. It was lit with candles and a small source of water trickled down into a rocky pool. There in the middle of the cavern was a tall wispy-looking man with a grey beard almost touching the floor. He was busy looking at something as they approached but hearing their step, swirled round, aiming his stick at them.

'Who goes there?' he called.

Gillimal stepped forward.

'It is I, Tirimae.'

The warlock lowered his weapon.

'Gillimal,' he exclaimed. 'I suspect you don't bring me any good news from the world above?'

'Actually I do,' Gillimal replied. 'Have you noticed my companion?'

'A boy?' the warlock questioned.

'THE boy,' Gillimal replied. 'The boy from the human world.'

What could be thought of as a small smile appeared to pass the warlock's lips, although it was so quick it could easily have been mistaken as a flicker of the light.

'Hmm,' he said. 'I know of your quest and your visit, the trees have been telling me. I cannot give you all that you come for but I can help in my own small way. You know of the loss of the acorn already, but did you know that the jewels from it have also been stolen?'

Gillimal gasped. 'The rubies too?'

'Indeed,' replied the warlock, 'and they must be found before the acorn can be returned to Tayrah otherwise it will be incomplete and your quest in vain! You must first travel north, where light nor day is ever at play, for the sun itself has been banished away.'

'He loves riddles,' whispered Gillimal. 'We must indulge him. To the shadow dwellers?' he questioned. 'What lies there?'

'The first ruby,' the warlock said gravely. 'I can say no more than this.'

'But that makes no sense,' Gillimal retorted. 'The dwellers are unable to leave the shadow lands, you know that.'

'Ah, that is what was told as truth,' the warlock replied, 'but actually there is a truth that lies deeper than that! The dwellers are cursed with living in darkness and they resent it. They found a means to travel undetected in the shadows of others, unseen yet seeing all. I have been led to believe that this has been practised many a year. It has made their acquiring a ruby quite possible.'

'Indeed,' said Gillimal thoughtfully. 'So we know our destination, what more can you tell us?'

'I know of some things you may need,' said the warlock, producing a bag from which he pulled a box. 'What do you see in here?' he asked Jeremy, opening the lid.

'I see nothing,' he replied, as the box looked quite empty.

'Exactly!' said Tirimae. 'And that is what others shall see when the contents of this box touches your skin. It will make you invisible! This may prove to be very useful. Take also this vial, it will lead you along the path of your quest. One drop in the source of any water will display its message. Take care though, to break the surface of the water once finished, as if not, the message is indestructible and could be seen by enemies. Finally, the black sun is ever watching and growing in strength. It is even now working against you and has released tonight a creature to seek you. It is sensing the boy's human blood. This can be disguised by the application of this cream each and every day. Do not forget!'

'Thank you my friend,' said Gillimal. 'As always, you show honour and bravery in your words. Thank you a thousand times.'

Gillimal bowed as the warlock said: 'Should you succeed upon your quest, Eringuild will once again be blessed.'

Gillimal returned the riddle by uttering, 'Hope is not gone whilst you remain, a saviour of our great nation's name!' The warlock smiled and bowed to Gillimal.

'Farewell friends and the bright sun be with you!' The Warlock watched the companions climb the steps once again until they were out of view, and hoped for the time that he would again rise to the world above.

7

Into the Land of the Shadow Dwellers

Gillimal rose again into the land of Eringuild, climbing the last of the steps before him with Jeremy at his heels, as the mountain entrance closed behind them. Jeremy turned his head to see the patch of grass exactly as it was before, with no sign that an opening had ever existed.

'Well,' said Gillimal, looking down the valley. 'We now know our direction, although I cannot say there is any pleasure in going there. We must sleep now, Jeremy, and travel at first light. It is a long journey to the shadow lands, with much travel to the north.'

Gillimal looked around him and walked towards a large tree trunk.

'This will do,' he said, and sat down just as a man

would with his back against the trunk. Jeremy had never slept out of his bed before and hesitated.

'Come,' said Gillimal, 'this is the most comfort we can expect tonight. Sit by my side and my fur will warm us both.'

Jeremy was also unused to such things as this and sat stiffly at Gillimal's side. The Asrah moved one arm gently around him and Jeremy soon found himself as comfortable and warm as he could be.

'Sleep now,' said Gillimal, 'and I shall keep watch. I will not let anything harm you.'

Jeremy closed his eyes, hearing only Gillimal's breathing as he fell to sleep.

*

The next morning they set off, having applied the magic balm to disguise Jeremy's human smell from whatever the black sun had sent to pursue him.

The shadow lands were as far in the north as Eringuild went and the closer they came to it, the gloomier it seemed. The sky was darkening even though Jeremy could still feel the sun's warmth on his back, and there seemed to be an eerie uncomfortable feeling that made one wish to turn round and head back.

By the time they had climbed the last mountain range, the air was full of damp and decay, making even breathing unpleasant. Gillimal instructed that they shuffle forward as low as they could to the ground and Jeremy peered over the ledge and gasped. What he saw before him was a wasteland, dark and dusty with no signs of any life, not even a blade of grass. The sky was thick with cloud, preventing any sunlight from peeping through, and Jeremy looked back at the sun in Eringuild, reassured that it was still there, bright as a star.

The land before him was dotted with mounds.

'Homes of the shadow dwellers,' Gillimal explained. 'The main population, that is. Any of importance live other there,' and he pointed to a pair of gates, black as the sky and equally intimidating. 'The Shadow dwellers take no chance,' Gillimal continued. 'They live in the rock, that is the king and any others he wants with him. That is where you must go.'

'Me!' Jeremy cried, suddenly alarmed. 'Are you not coming too?'

'The potion will not hide both of us, I will be here waiting for you. You must have faith in yourself, Jeremy. You are more powerful than you know.'

'But how shall I find the ruby when I'm inside?'

'He is a clever king,' said Gillimal thoughtfully. 'I imagine it will be somewhere so open that it appears secret, rather somewhere none would think he would be foolish enough to keep it, therein lies the cunning!'

At this, Gillimal opened the box from Tirimae and gently blew some of the contents onto Jeremy. It fell first on his arm and he watched in awe as it disappeared before his eyes.

'Remember,' said Gillimal, 'despite them not seeing you, the shadow dwellers have other strong senses. Move swiftly but as light as a feather. Find the ruby and retreat to me.'

Jeremy nodded and then realised that Gillimal

could not see any actions anymore.

'Yes Gillimal,' he said, and began his descent down the hill.

As he approached the gates, Jeremy realised their true size. Enormous and daunting, they towered above him, making him feel suddenly afraid. There was not a being in sight and he slipped through and down the tunnel behind. This was lit with candles, releasing a small, dim glow into the surrounding darkness. Jeremy lost all sense of time but arrived eventually in what seemed to be a throne room, and there in the dimming light of the cavern, he saw several hooded figures surrounding a long wooden table. Inside their hoods seemed only blackness and their long, thin fingers seemed more like bone than flesh.

At the head of the table, sat the king of the shadow lands. Perched on his throne, which was carved with various figures, they were obviously in the middle of some great discussion and Jeremy crept closer to hear their words.

'So,' said the shadow king in a dry, crackly voice. 'You all know our position. Our designs have long since been set in motion. The alliance with the tall ones was tactical and necessary and being as dissatisfied as us, they were easy to manipulate. Furthermore, their power lies in brute force and not mind, making them no real threat to us!'

The other dwellers nodded and some appeared to snigger.

'The plot has been carried out and the acorn stolen from the castle of Tayrah. Only I and the giant king know its position but I can assure you I know its location. I walked in his shadow to see it done. With the acorn dislodged and peace along with it, Eringuild is free to attack. No more will we be banished and exiled to the perimeters of the land, we shall invade and take sole reign over all. Any denying us will be easily dealt with.'

'But my liege,' questioned another, 'forgive me but how can we invade when the sun shines so brightly?'

At this point the shadow king removed his hood, showing a terrifying face, scaled like a dragon and hard as bones. He was smiling in such a way that made Jeremy tremble.

'Ah, my lord,' he cackled. 'You are right to question so, but did I not say that the giants were stupid? The acorn was taken as instructed with its location known only to me. But this is war and nothing can be left to chance. Ruling with the giants would be an acceptable price for power, but ruling solely, that would be even greater! Without the giant lord knowing, I stole a ruby from the acorn and have it here in my possession!'

The king then paused in order to hear the many sighs of admiration.

'The lack of the acorn invites war but without the rubies, the symbol is redundant and everlasting night shall fall when the black sun consumes the evil one. Who best to rule then my lords, when the whole of Eringuild is covered in darkness?'

'Will they not act to prevent this?' questioned a dweller.

'Undoubtedly,' smiled the king, 'but it will be an insignificant attempt against the power of the black sun. These other creatures need their light; they cannot exist fully without it. Watch them suffer and fade, like broken souls they will be fully manageable and will bend easily to our all-consuming power!'

'You are a great king indeed!' chanted the other dwellers. 'Soon they will all pay and the power of the dark one will rise!'

They all clacked horribly together until the king said, 'Leave me now, I wish to be alone.'

The others bowed and left at the far end of the room. Jeremy noticed with horror that they had no feet and merely glided across the floor, leaving no print or mark.

The king waved his bony hand as they passed and the room quickly became empty. He rose from his throne and looked back down the passage through which the lords had left. There was no trace of them now. He returned to his throne and kneeling in front whilst looking carefully around, began tapping the wood. As he did so, a hollow sound could be heard amongst the many dense taps and with a twist, a piece came off in his hands, displaying a small hole. The king reached inside and pulled out a bright red shape, placing it on the table in front of him. Such was its brightness that it cast a red glow over his face, but rather than softening it, seemed to intensify the hardened features to make them even more frightening. *The ruby!* Thought Jeremy. *He keeps it in his throne!* The king held the ruby in his hands for a while and then replaced it in the chair, screwing the wood in place again to conceal it.

He then rose and glided across the room, heading down the same tunnel his lords had left. Jeremy froze, listening hard, but all he could hear was silence.

He was terrified the king would return but knew he must go down into the room and take the ruby from the throne. He crept with the silence of a mouse and yet walked swiftly down the table to the throne. He didn't need to tap the wood, remembering exactly where the hole had appeared. Like magic, he twisted the wood in his fingers and soon he was clasping the first of the stolen rubies. Concealing it quickly in his trouser pocket, Jeremy replaced the wood and headed back to his original position. As he turned back once more, he saw now with horror that the shadow king had returned and was sniffing the air like a bloodhound.

'There has been a stranger here,' he called in a mocking tone. Jeremy didn't dare breathe. 'And I believe that he is here still,' called the king, gliding round the table.

'Strangers are not welcome here!' he continued. 'Especially those that conceal themselves. I can smell you,' he whispered, 'your fear is dripping from you. Perhaps you should see the full force of whom you are dealing with.' He shed his robes, displaying his awful body, scaled and bony like his face with claw-like fingers and black holes for eyes.

'Do you see me, stranger?' the king called, and Jeremy put his hand across his mouth to stop himself screaming but it was too late. A small sound left his lips and the king instantly turned to it. Despite being invisible, Jeremy felt certain he could be seen, as the eyes of the shadow king seemed to burn through him. He turned and fled down the passageway, hearing the king call, 'Guards, guards!' behind him.

Jeremy had never run so fast in his life and reached the entrance to the rock in record time. He could hear the muffled calls of his enemies behind him and ran across the dusty wasteland clumsily towards the ledge where he had left Gillimal. As he ran, he saw with horror that the dwellers had reached the entrance and had spotted his footprints in the dust. They came after him, brandishing what looked like large marbles. They began to throw these strategically and as soon as they hit the ground, the contents burst with a bomb-like effect, exploding around Jeremy. He screamed in terror and managed simultaneously to call for Gillimal. The Asrah's head appeared over the ledge and he came running at full speed. The dwellers were now almost upon Jeremy, reaching out their bony fingers to grasp him.

Gillimal jumped the last stretch of the hill, a gigantic leap both graceful and accurate, landing in front of Jeremy, who was now almost completely exposed and cowering in Gillimal's shadow.

Gillimal rose up to his full height, lifting his head into the air and the dwellers stopped before him. They dared not come any closer but hissed and spat from the position they held, forming a tight semi-circle. They suddenly parted and the king glided forward, his hood now covering his face again.

'What is your business here, Asrah?' snarled the king. 'You have neither purpose nor invite, and what is this creature you carry with you?'

'My business is my own,' replied Gillimal. 'As is my companion.'

'You refuse me answers?' demanded the king.

'When you are surrounded by my soldiers with thousands more at my call?'

'Your men cower with good reason,' said Gillimal pointedly. 'Or have you forgotten the fighting of old? We battled with your ancestors centuries ago, when we discovered that even a skin as hard as yours can be broken.'

'Suppose I take you by force?' suggested the shadow king.

'Indeed,' said Gillimal, 'suppose then I release the information of your new travelling skills. That breaks the treaty of peace, does it not, and all Eringuild would unite against you. War you would have, but not on your own terms.'

Although Gillimal did not speak altogether plainly, the king understood his meaning perfectly. As much as he would have loved to fight Gillimal, he was a clever king and could see that wining a battle would not be worth losing a war. This would not help his current plans and so must be disregarded.

After what seemed like an agonising pause, the shadow king waved his arm, signalling his troops to retreat. 'Go,' he called to Gillimal, 'but know that setting foot here again will be your last tread in Eringuild!'

The troops headed back to the rocks and Jeremy watched them anxiously, half expecting it to be a trap and the full force of the shadow dwellers to return. Gillimal remained in his position and watched them also. From the dwellers troops, an advisor next to the king said, 'My lord, surely we will not let them walk away like this?'

'Silence!' ordered the king. 'Do not question my judgements: my actions have strengthened our cause. Besides, there is more than one way to conquer an enemy.' And he smiled his eerie smile.

That night in his throne room, the king instructed his advisors to draw a black circle around him. That was then surrounded with candles and symbols of old. The king knelt in the circle, facing what seemed like a large window in the rock, covered with wooden shutters. In front of him was a clay bowl, into which he poured a liquid from a vial and scratched a scale from his arm. As he mixed the two together, they started to bubble and fizz. The king instructed that the windows in front of him be opened and as they were, the black sun could be seen in the sky, huge and daunting to behold. The king drank the mixture and spoke to the sun in a language never heard before. It seemed a mixture of snarls and clicks and foreign words but translated roughly as this:

'Oh dark one, hear us in our time of need. We worship you and wait anxiously for the fullness of your power. Obstruct those that stand against us. Make them suffer, fail their cause, we entreat you!'

The black sun remained motionless as the shadow king bowed before it, until the surface of one of the craters appeared to ripple and a shape could be witnessed underneath, clawing at what kept it prisoner.

From the sun itself came forth a terrifying noise – a shrieking howl, provoking thoughts of despair and chaos. The king laughed heartily, cackling with pleasure. A great wind then came up, whipping round and extinguishing all of the candles.

The room was thrown into darkness except for the eyes of the shadow king, which seemed now to burn as red as blood.

*

Meanwhile, Gillimal and Jeremy had hastily crossed back into Eringuild, leaving the borders of the shadow lands behind them. Jeremy had never been so relieved to see the sun before and the light it shone on the world. His thoughts were only temporarily darkened by witnessing the black sun, seemingly now just a little bigger in the sky. They came upon a forest and walked a little way in, pausing to rest awhile by a small pond.

'I'm sorry if I disappointed you, Gillimal,' said Jeremy gravely. 'I did truly try my best but he frightened me.'

Gillimal turned to his small companion and smiled. 'That is only to be expected, my human friend. I warned you that much you saw here would do so, but you did well, Jeremy – very well. You fulfilled your purpose. May I see the ruby?'

Jeremy had completely forgotten about the jewel in his panic with the shadow dwellers and reached inside his pocket, carefully bringing it out and cradling it in the palm of his hand. He held it out to Gillimal who sighed.

'I cannot tell you the years that have passed since I have seen this sight,' he said. 'The Asrahs have always fought to keep the peace in Eringuild, throughout the centuries, and we have always succeeded until now.'

'Thank you for saving me earlier,' Jeremy said. 'I couldn't have escaped without you. You were so fearsome to them.'

'The Asrahs were all warriors once,' said Gillimal. 'Trained to fight and protect these lands. That was our purpose at first but now we are protectors in a more peaceful way. Yet I have to admit that the old ways still live within me. I have not felt that fire in my blood for a long time. But my friend, we linger too long. Our quest is far from complete. Take the vial from Tirimae and let one drop fall into the pond over there. It will advise us of our next course. Remember to wipe the surface of the water afterwards, we do not want any followers, do we?'

Jeremy shook his head and did as Gillimal instructed. The drop seemed to sink like a heavy bubble beneath the water and then rise again, exploding on the surface. Words began to form, moving with the lapping of the water and this is what Jeremy read:

From shadow lands to marshes go, for what you seek is far below.

Hidden in the watery blue,
Is one who holds a message for you.

'What does it mean?' questioned Jeremy.

'It talks of the marshlands,' said Gillimal. 'They lie to the south of Tayrah and are home to the Glubin nation.'

'Glubins?' Jeremy asked. 'What are those?'

Gillimal smiled. 'Once seen they are not easily forgotten. Come, Jeremy, we must be on our way.

Wipe the surface of the pond and we'll depart.'

Gillimal walked away, leaving Jeremy still knelt by the pool of water. Perhaps it was his age or his inexperience in such matters but Jeremy a little too carelessly brushed his hand against the surface of the water and joined Gillimal. As the companions departed, a few words of the clue could just be seen moving with the motion of the water.

It was only a few hours later that two creatures approached the pond where Jeremy and Gillimal had sat. The first creature resembled that of a giant wolf with blood-red eyes and shaggy black fur. It stalked towards the pond, sniffing the surrounding area and suddenly let forth a blood-curdling howl. It had caught a human scent, faint now but still traceable, and it dribbled with the excitement of the chase and the prize to come. Its companion was more man-like in form. It was a tall figure, hooded like a shadow dweller but yet not one. Had there been others around them, they would have smelt a strange smell of decay in the air, such a smell that might be given off by one not quite living. In the fading hours of daylight, the remains of the message was still just readable. As the figure read the inscription, it inhaled deeply and the words seemed to dissolve into golden strands and drift up its nose and into its body where they cast a golden glow. This was the second being to be spewed from the black sun, following the prayers of the shadow king. Deadlier than the first by its cunning and intelligence, its power was to ingest any words that may aid its quest, placing them into an internal jigsaw in its mind to form any clues to the whereabouts of the companions or the acorn. The beast padded to the pond and sat beside the figure, who now rose to its feet. Looking at the animal, the figure grinned a grin both revolting and terrifying to see and uttered the two words: 'Glubin Town.'

8

Glubin Town

Glubin Town was the kind of place you would never believe in until you had seen it, and could never forget once you had, as Jeremy discovered as they entered the marshlands. It could be best described as a nest of humorous chaos, bustling and busy as a small town but the action of the area took place down by the marshes themselves, where a jetty was covered in lounging Glubins. Lazy by nature, they spent most of their time in this location, heckling for trade and smoking the marsh weed in long pipes.

'Pennies for dem favours!' they would call at passers-by, running errands in the water for small change.

A Glubin, Jeremy found, was a frog-like creature, except it walked on two legs and did not hop. They came approximately up to Jeremy's waist in height and whilst charming you with words, were not against slipping their slimy fingers into your pockets.

'Tell them nothing they don't need to know,' said Gillimal. 'They are harmless enough but our business is still best between us.'

As they walked down the jetty, surrounded by the water of the marshes, Glubins were everywhere. Lying against barrels and playing card games, they called out to the strangers, angling for trade. Gillimal seemed to have a particular Glubin in mind and rejected all offers with civility, searching the jetty. Then a change in his stride took place and he moved purposefully towards a certain spot, where a particularly cheeky-looking Glubin was lounging about.

'Stubb,' called Gillimal softly, and the Glubin turned around.

'Hey!' he exclaimed, his face lighting into a sickly smile. 'Tis dat Asrah! And who be dat friend?'

The Glubin stood and sidled up to Jeremy, placing a sticky arm round his waist.

'Ah,' said Gillimal sternly. 'None of your tricks, Stubb.' He noticed well-practiced fingers stretching for Jeremy's trouser pocket.

'Me no do nothing!' said the Glubin in the broken English that was common in the region.

'We need a favour,' said Gillimal directly.

'Penny for dem favours,' smiled the Glubin, and held out a green hand.

Gillimal produced a local coin and the Glubin flicked it up in the air and then inspected it, rolling it about in his fingers.

'Well now,' said the Glubin, concealing the coin somewhere about his body, 'now dat business be dun, what be dem pleasure?'

'What do the fish say at the moment?' said Gillimal.

'Oh, dis and dat,' said the Glubin slyly. 'Who know dem fishes? They see all.'

Gillimal tried a different tack.

'Has anything unusual happened lately?' he questioned.

'Well…' said the Glubin, stretching his legs so that they dangled in the water. 'There was dat man…'

'Which man?' said Gillimal.

'More favours, more pennies,' said the Glubin pointedly, and sighing, Gillimal tossed another coin his way.

'Well,' said the Glubin, slowly.

'Oh do get on with it,' snapped Gillimal, growing impatient. 'What of this man?'

'Slowly, softly,' said the Glubin. 'You need to be cool like dem marsh breeze! Have a puff o' old marshy, she set you right!'

Gillimal shook his head, so the pipe was offered to Jeremy.

'Shame on you!' exclaimed Gillimal. 'You should be no more offering pipes to that child than one of your own glublets!'

'Dem fine,' shrugged the Glubin, 'and they grow to be fine too! Anyways,' he continued. 'Der I was, smoking that pipe and sitting a while when me decided to talk to dem fishes. We was chatting away when a shadow appeared over dem water. Me saw a face, dat man me saw and he was jerky. No smoking of dat happy pipe for him. He looked dim scared for dim life, like something be chasin' 'im and then from dat hand of his, he let something drop. It was an accident; me sure as he clawed at them waters, but dem ting did sink. Me be watching from under dem waters and me saw dem flash of red. Me went to collect dem ting but Magdela, she too be watchin' and grabbed dem ting to her cave. Der it be still, and dat all me know.'

Gillimal barely showed a flicker of interest at the story but said calmly, 'I see…'

'Dat it?' questioned the Glubin. 'Dat all after me story?'

'A good tale,' said Gillimal. 'I need to think and rest a while. We'll be back at sundown and may further require your services.'

'Water favours?' questioned the Glubin, and Gillimal nodded.

'Oh no!' said the Glubin. 'I no do water favours after dem sun gone down. Dem marshes not just full of dem Glubins and me like to see what comin'!'

'All right, later then,' said Gillimal. 'Back here in an hour.'

'So it be!' said the Glubin, and Gillimal and Jeremy walked back along the jetty with the beady Glubin eyes watching their every move.

*

When they were sitting in privacy, shortly after their meeting with the Glubin, Gillimal expressed his true feelings.

'This is good news!' he exclaimed. 'That shape the Glubin mentioned is most likely to be the second ruby.'

'So now we know where it is,' said Jeremy. 'Can we go and get it?'

'That is where it becomes more difficult,' said the Asrah. 'Magdela he spoke of is a water witch. She dislikes the world above the water and rarely surfaces. She is one of the fears that the Glubin spoke of. He will send a message to her for us before dark but we must think of something to make her visit worthwhile. She will not readily hand over the ruby, especially if she finds out we are seeking it. We must be ready to bargain, Jeremy, and find something she herself would desire. Let us look at the local markets and visit again our friend Glubin to send the message and arrange the meeting.'

In all this excitement, Jeremy had not given any thought to the man mentioned in the story or who he was, but as he would later discover, when truth was told, there had only ever been one human in Eringuild before himself and he bore the initials H.A. – Henry Applegate.

9

The Water Witch

A short while later, the companions returned to the jetty, without an item to tempt the water witch. Having searched the local market, crawling with Glubins, there had been nothing that Gillimal thought suitable for the task.

Tired and exasperated, Gillimal turned to Jeremy and said, 'Time is running out, my friend. We must speak with Magdela tonight and if we delay any further, the Glubin will not run the errand – the hours of sunlight are quickly fading!'

They found the hapless Glubin, in almost the same position they had left him, smoking a fresh pipe of marsh weed and dangling one leg carelessly in the water.

'Ah! Dem friends return. What be dem favour?' the Glubin asked.

'We wish to speak with Magdela,' replied Gillimal. 'Please send word for her to meet with us here tonight and tell her Gillimal of the Asrahs asks for her.'

'Oh dat is no pretty favour,' said the Glubin. 'Me no trust Magdela, she bad water witch!'

'If you're angling for further pennies, rest assured we have them,' said Gillimal bluntly.

'Why did dem not say so before?' exclaimed the Glubin. 'Holdem dem pipe.' Thrusting his pipe into Jeremy's hand, he leapt with a splash into the marsh water and disappeared beneath the surface.

'What do we do now?' questioned Jeremy.

'We wait,' said Gillimal, sitting down.

'And what do we do when she gets here, Gillimal?' Jeremy questioned further.

'Leave that to me,' said the Asrah. 'You must wait in the bushes for safety. If all goes to plan, we shall be holding the second ruby very shortly.'

The hours of sunlight faded and the companions were still waiting on the pier. Local Glubins came to light lamps at intervals along the jetty, casting glowing reflections into the water. Jeremy rose, as his legs had gone to sleep, and looked at Gillimal. He was dozing with his head slightly inclined towards his body and Jeremy, wishing not to wake him, tiptoed to the jetty's edge and peered over into the water.

It was still and dark, not even a ripple. *I hope nothing has hurt the Glubin,* Jeremy thought. *I do like that little fellow.*

Gillimal gave a snort in his sleep, sending a puff of air out into the chill night. Jeremy turned his head at the noise and when he again looked back at the water, gave a scream, as a face was staring back at him from beneath the surface. Not his own reflection, a woman's face, with swirls of long black hair and a cunning smile on her lips. Gillimal woke at the noise and Jeremy ran to the safety of the bushes, just as the creature rose from the depths, having only just caught a fleeting glance of Jeremy. She was mostly the shape of a woman but with gills and fins like a fish. *I wonder if she has always looked this way,* Jeremy thought to himself, as he peered from the branches.

Despite her appearance, he now felt no fear. The creature of course was Magdela, risen from her watery cave, and she, eying the one visible companion, warily spoke.

'Much time has passed since I surfaced from the depths, Gillimal of the Asrahs,' she said. 'What creature hides from me?'

'None that concerns you,' the Asrah replied.

She looked around her. 'Has the world changed so much since you and I last met so many years ago?'

'The land is much as it always was,' replied Gillimal, 'but the times are approaching those of war, I am sad to say.'

'The world and I are not so close kin,' she replied haughtily. 'It concerns itself not with me, nor I with it. What do you wish of me, Gillimal? I am sure you must want something?'

Her question was interrupted by another splash and there appeared the Glubin. Clambering onto the jetty, he called proudly, 'Here dem be, here dem be, I got her, de water witch from the depths, me brought

ANNIE MUSCUTT

her for you. Now,' he said holding out his green fingers, 'where be dem pennies?'

Gillimal quickly filled his hand with the coins and the Glubin bowed.

'So what be dem business here?'

'Our business is not your concern,' said Gillimal shortly. 'Leave us be please and enjoy your new coins.'

'Steady Asrah, remember cool like dem breeze!' said the Glubin, and walking a wide step round Magdela, he disappeared up the jetty.

'My apologies,' said Gillimal, 'the Glubins lie short of many qualities, not least their manners.'

'We all have our purpose,' breathed Magdela. 'And so, Gillimal, I ask you again, what is yours?'

She fixed her eyes upon the Asrah, waiting for his answer.

'The Glubins tell of an item you may recently have found, it belongs to me and I would kindly ask you to return it.'

Jeremy looked at Gillimal, confused by his new strategy.

'And why should I do that?' questioned the water witch. 'You are seeking it, so it must be of some worth. It sits even now in my treasure trove, deep down under the water. Perhaps I am not inclined to return it, what say you to that?'

Gillimal replied but Jeremy was not listening, or be to be more accurate, he did not hear. He saw the Asrah's mouth move but heard no words.

A strange feelings had come over him, a feeling

50

that he was somehow connected to this creature and must speak with her. Whilst thinking this, he had emerged from the bushes, where he had been previously hiding, and now walked slowly towards the water witch, edging closer to her, one shuffle at a time, until he was almost able to touch her. She saw him first out of the corner of her eye and flicked her head quickly to look fully upon him, gazing with a mixed expression of surprise and sorrow.

'Who are you?' she whispered.

'My name is Jeremy,' he replied. 'Why do you look at me in that way?'

'I have met one such as you before,' she continued, 'but it was long ago and is now surrounded by sadness.'

'I make you sad, don't I?' Jeremy questioned, and she nodded.

'I have not seen one such as you in Eringuild since the last and you reminded me of him.'

'I'm sad too,' Jeremy said. 'I have lost someone as well and I'm trying to find him again.'

He put his head on one side and continued speaking, although it was now more to himself than to her, as thoughts began to appear inside his head.

'You're hiding away from what you remember,' he continued, 'because you think it won't hurt you anymore if you can try and forget. I think you are hiding, just like I did at home, hiding with your secret. You didn't chose to leave the world, did you? You're just hiding from it.'

The witch looked at him; she was quite still apart

from the trembling of her hands.

'Talk to me,' said Jeremy, 'and maybe I can help.'

Whilst Gillimal looked on with spellbound curiosity, the witch motioned for Jeremy to look into the water. As the tears fell from her eyes, they created a moving picture. Magdela was gazing up through the water at someone. Someone standing at the edge with his back to her. As the figure turned round, Jeremy uttered a muffled cry as he recognised the face of his father. His own dear daddy! Then the pictures changed and his father was gone. Magdela appeared again and again, but not him. The picture faded and Jeremy felt that he now understood. He was not the only one who felt they had lost his father.

'I had left the world,' she sighed now. 'It was so unfriendly and sad, I preferred to be alone. It was not an easy change to make and occasionally I felt the need to return to the surface. I never saw anything that made me want to rise until that day. As I raised my head from the water, I saw him. A creature I had never seen before – no creature of Eringuild, I was sure. He had his back to me and was holding something in his hands. The motion of the water startled him and he turned round. For a moment only I saw his face, so kind and serious, but I was afraid to stay and took myself back under the waves. Many times I returned to the surface, almost always glimpsing him. I returned to my cave on those days with the only feeling of happiness I've ever felt. As I became bolder, I went further towards the shore and finding we could understand each other, held short conversations. He talked of Eringuild but never of himself. After a while, he would begin to get restless and say he needed to go and I would wait patiently for him to return again.'

Her eyes filled with tears as she said: 'Then he disappeared.' The water witch sobbed. 'I waited for so long, returning to the surface again and again, searching the horizon, but I never saw him again. Not until that day when I glimpsed him above the water, the day something dropped from his hands. I swam up to the surface, daring to hope, but it was too late and he had disappeared again. The object had disappeared too, sinking down into the depths, but I traced it and took it to my home. I felt it was a little piece of him and all now that I had left to hold onto.'

Jeremy's eyes had grown wide throughout this tale, not quite believing his ears.

'You knew my daddy,' Jeremy said, and his own eyes started to well up with tears.

'That was your father?' she questioned, and the little boy nodded. An understanding had now been forged between them. Both looked at the other until Jeremy said: 'When I was a very little boy, my daddy went missing. Not from this world but from the world I come from. I never understood where he went and nobody at home would talk about him so I could never ask. Now I know he's here in Eringuild, I can bring him back, I know I can! But I can't do it alone, Magdela, I need your help. Please give me what my father dropped into the water that day.'

She looked unsure, unwilling to give up her treasured reminder of him. Jeremy continued gently. 'If you will help me, I promise to bring my father to see you again, just as it used to be.'

The witch looked at him and smiled a sad smile. 'You are so little but so strong,' she said. 'Strong like him. Wait for me a moment, I will return.'

She dived under the water and rising moments later, clutched something in her hand. Washing it in the waters around her, she then held it out, unfolding her fingers to display the second ruby. Handing it carefully to Jeremy, she said, 'I hope that you find all that you seek.'

'Thank you Magdela,' he said. 'You have been kind to me, and my daddy shall know it.'

He didn't know what else to say and so shyly planted a kiss on her cheek.

'You have a friend in me, little one,' she said. 'If ever you need me, call out my name, I shall always hear you.' And with that, the smiling Magdela disappeared beneath the waves.

The companions were again alone with only the lapping of the water around them. Jeremy looked again at the ruby and smiled up at Gillimal, who now kneeled before him.

'Such a little boy,' he said, 'to hold so much power. You are wise, my human friend, as well as strong. You showed me tonight what my many centuries in Eringuild have not. You are of greatness, Jeremy, and the Asrahs will speak of you throughout time.'

10

Thoughts of Home

As he lay trying to sleep that evening, Jeremy's thoughts were still of the water witch. Despite lying in a bed for the first time since arriving in Eringuild and feeling similar comforts to those of his own home, Jeremy could not seem to rest. The day's events kept playing through his mind. He felt for Magdela, recognising a similar pain to his own, when his father disappeared. He imagined her watching him from afar like in a fairy tale, surfacing from the water to gaze upon him. To think of him so fondly only for him to vanish without a trace! He pictured her surfacing now to empty shores, deserted and lonely. Now he thought about it, she had found his father just as he and his mother had lost him. And now he was gone again! These thoughts then led him to think about his mother, for the first time since entering Eringuild. He felt a sudden panic that she would be searching for him, mad with worry and grief, without any understanding of his disappearance. This prompted him to whisper to Gillimal, who was watching out of the window.

'Gillimal?' he called softly, and the Asrah turned to look at him. 'I was thinking about my mother, she'll be worried sick after all this time.'

'Set your mind at rest, Jeremy. The times, along with many other things, are different from world to world. Your world has its own time, as we have ours. As you entered Eringuild, the time in your world froze and it will continue from where it left, as soon as you go back. Do you understand?'

'I think so,' said Jeremy slowly. 'So Mother can't worry because she doesn't realise I'm gone yet?'

'Precisely,' said Gillimal. 'So you may sleep easy in that knowledge.'

Jeremy still could not sleep. 'But there's another thing, Gillimal,' he continued, and the Asrah looked at him patiently. 'I thought you said that creatures in Eringuild had to stay within their own lands and couldn't leave unless they were invited, so how can you travel from land to land?'

'That is simple,' said Gillimal. 'The Asrahs are the protectors of Eringuild as you know, and have the freedom to live where we choose. We have no land of our own and pass from place to place as we patrol. That is understood by all occupants of Eringuild and is accepted as the way things are.'

'I see,' said Jeremy. 'What will we do next, Gillimal?'

'We must go down to the water at first light to

read the next sign,' the Asrah continued. 'We do not want the company of the Glubins and rising early will ensure that. We can then slip away unnoticed before they even realise we're gone.'

11

The First Battle

In the early hours of the morning, the two companions returned to the water's edge. The sun was just rising, casting a golden glow over Eringuild. But it did not stand alone in the sky, there too was the black sun, cold and hard, almost doubled in size since last seen. Gillimal observed the worry on Jeremy's face.

'Do not fear,' he said reassuringly, 'it will only sense it. Our sun still rises and in that is hope.'

Holding the vial, Jeremy poured a drop into the water as before and a new message appeared. Before he could read it though, he felt the hair on his neck bristle and the jetty beneath him groan with the weight of something huge. Gillimal too had sensed this change and swung round to see the cause. There, stalking down the jetty, was the enormous black wolf, with each paw as big as Jeremy's head. It had fixed its eyes on the boy, dribbling with anticipation. Jeremy felt absolute panic and his heart showed it in its frightened beating. Gillimal stood in its path.

'Go back to where you came from,' he roared, 'whilst you still have the chance!'

The wolf snarled but did not cease its heavy step. Gillimal searched around him, he had no weapon to protect Jeremy and so held up his head and uttered a deep bellow that rang out through the surrounding area. It was a call any Asrah would know well and signalled the need for help. Gillimal prepared to battle, standing at his full height, when a strange thing occurred. As the creature came forth, in front of it on the jetty sprang from the water an army of Glubins with Stubb as the leader. They had heard Gillimal's call and ventured up to the surface to find out its meaning. They were armed with what looked like miniature catapults with pebbles as shots.

Stubb jumped forward onto the jetty and addressing the wolf, said, 'You leave dem that boy be!' and fired his catapult, hitting the wolf squarely on the nose. It yelped and then looked up as a wave of pebbles came towards it, fired by every available Glubin. The wolf staggered back, hit again and again by the sharp sting of the pebbles. It attempted to snap at any nearby foe but they just dived back into the water for safety. The wolf, infused with anger, sprinted forward, leaping at Gillimal with claws outstretched. The Asrah stood his ground and the two tussled as they collided. The wolf was a symbol of destruction and was pleased to cause pain to anyone, but its real target was Jeremy and so knocking Gillimal into the water with a swipe of its claw, it lurched forward again towards its victim.

Jeremy bolted as fast as his legs would carry him down the jetty with the wolf hot in pursuit. But like all jetties, Jeremy soon came to its end and turned to face his attacker. The wolf paused for a moment, eying him up and down. It was a hunter after all and there was as much pleasure in the chase, as in the kill itself.

As it paused, the Glubins made one final attempt to help and Stubb, leaping bravely, grabbed the wolf's tail with other Glubins holding on too, forming a chain. The rest made whips from the water reeds, which delivered stinging blows to their enemy. The wolf swirled round angrily, trying to catch its tail, together with those holding it and Stubb called to his fellows, 'Be brave, dem Glubins! Hold fast as dis end be the safer one!'

Jeremy watched with horror as the tiny creatures fought bravely for him and then suddenly a thought came to him.

'Magdela!' he cried out in a piercing voice, that he had never had cause to use in his life before. All of a sudden, there was a rumble in the water and the jetty began to shake. The wolf only just had time to look around it in bewilderment, as a split second later, out of the water came the witch, her eyes blazing with fury. She looped over the jetty, grabbing the wolf by its fur and diving back into the water on the other side with it and all attached. The water frothed and bubbled as the struggle took place with only glimpses of fur and fins occasionally seen.

Finally all was quiet and the water lay still. Jeremy got down on his hands and knees, peering anxiously into the water. First came Stubb, panting with the excitement of it all.

'Dem boy, dem boy,' he called, heaving himself up onto the jetty. 'Me NEVER be doin' dat again! Glubins be built for swimming and puffin' but not fightin'!'

He collapsed in mock exhaustion on the jetty just as Magdela rose and swam to the edge of the pier. Jeremy ran and threw his arms around her.

'There, there,' she said. 'It's all over now.'

As they embraced, Gillimal came down the jetty, limping but otherwise unhurt.

'Here dem be!' called Stubb. 'Where you been, Asrah? You been missing all dem fun!' he said provokingly.

Gillimal glared until Jeremy turned and laughed. Quietly at first and then louder, he was so relieved to be alive. Gillimal's frown became a smile.

'It seems to me that there is more to a Glubin than meets the eye!' he said. 'Who would have thought there was a warrior in you, Stubb!'

'Oh, me do nothing,' said the Glubin modestly, but smiled a secret smile.

Gillimal joined the group and said, 'Come, friends. Let us read our next sign, we must be moving on.'

Jeremy instinctively reached for Tirimae's box but Gillimal stopped him.

'We needn't worry about your lotion now, my friend. For that particular part of this tale is done.

12

Messages in the Water

As Stubb and Magdela departed, Gillimal and Jeremy stood over the water and poured a magical drop from the vial. As before, a message appeared and the companions both stooped to the water's edge in order to read it. Perhaps it was their concentration upon this or the overwhelming events of the early day, but neither party was aware that they were being most carefully watched. This was of course by the companion to the wolf. He had been in his current position for quite some time and had witnessed the entire battle. Had he felt it would have been within his own best interests to assist the wolf, he would have readily done so, but sensing that particular party was not going to be victorious, had merely watched on from the shadows. He watched now still, thinking hard about the situation.

He had clearly underestimated the opposition. The

wolf had been one of the most fearsome of the black sun's followers but yet had been so easily beaten by a mere boy and a band of friends. He decided a change of tactics was needed. His purpose remained the same: to obstruct Jeremy in any way possible and bring Eringuild to destruction, but he now held the advantage of knowing their whereabouts and being able to follow them onwards. It was the ability to think that made this enemy ten times as dangerous as the last.

The wolf had been a symbol of the black sun's strength but this creature was more of its mind, its black ability to think with cunning and deception, whilst maintaining its lust for cruelty and pain. He realised that it was outnumbered at present and certainly the water witch would readily return if called, so a second attack would not be a clever move.

However, he thought, smiling, *this boy can now be followed and observed and without him having the smallest clue. He will unwittingly be leading me to the acorn. From there, it shall be quickly snatched at first chance and all their efforts will be for nothing!*

So he decided, killing Jeremy was no longer the chief objective, rather keeping him alive to aid his other purpose: finding the acorn and preventing its return to Tayrah by any means necessary.

The companions were completely unaware this plotting was so close to them, hidden only by the shadow in which the creature lay. They were engrossed in reading the next message:

Where laughter and happiness turn to dread,
And many nations fear to tread,
For though we be brave, or strong or tall,
We still shall be the smallest of all!

'It speaks of the Giant Kingdom,' said Gillimal with a tone of surprise in his voice. 'That is not what I was expecting. Let me think of what we know already. The shadow king formed an allegiance with the giants but this new information suggests that the acorn must be concealed within Giant Country. I would never have imagined the shadow king would allow it, despite his stealing of a ruby!'

Gillimal bowed his head in thought, closing his eyes.

'Something is not right,' he said. 'But my mind is clouded.'

Suddenly his head rose again with renewed vigour. 'That's it!' he exclaimed. 'For the shadow king to trust the location of the acorn, he must have been able to see its hiding place at all times. There is only one place it can be... Dowentide! The giant's mountain! So tall it is visible from the boundaries of the shadow lands despite it being on the southernmost side of Eringuild. We have our direction, Jeremy. Let's make haste, for unless I am very much mistaken, the acorn is now within our reach!'

13

Whispers on the Wind

News had a way of travelling in Eringuild and that evening, through the means of all that was dark in the country, the message of the wolf's demise came back to the shadow king. To us, we would have seen no more than a wisp of breeze whip around his bony head but something spoke to him, whispering secrets in his ear. The king had been boiling with anger and resentment since his meeting with Gillimal and that cursed boy! To add most hateful insult to injury, he then found the precious ruby missing and realised the true purpose of Jeremy's visit to his land. He had been deceived! But a different feeling overcame him now, one that had been a stranger for most of his existence. It was that of fear – a deep, hollow fear that swelled through his body like an illness, spreading a sense of dread. This was not how it was supposed to be! The boy should be dead by now, yet the black sun's strongest warrior had not succeeded in the task.

Instead they were moving closer and closer to his undoing, and if they succeeded, his great plans would be but a distant memory in the passage of time. This opportunity for a shift of power would be unlikely ever to occur again and it was with this thought in mind the king decided that he, lord of the shadow lands, would travel under cloak of darkness to the giant country and seize the acorn himself! He knew they already held one ruby and was most fearful that they now held a second. If they should locate the acorn as well, all would be lost, but not if it were in the shadow lands. Even if an army of Eringuild invaded them, it would be too late. The black sun would consume and everything would fall under its shadow.

The king was resolute and prepared to travel. Clapping his scaly hands, a minion appeared. 'Prepare me a shadow horse,' the king commanded, 'the fastest you can find. We leave at once!'

14

Travel to the Giant Lands

Gillimal and Jeremy continued their journey away from Glubin Town and towards the giant country. Since beginning their quest, they had travelled to the far north to the shadow lands and then back to the central regions of Glubin Town, and now must go to the south and the farthest reaches of Eringuild. As they walked, Gillimal had the distinct impression that they were being followed. All the animal elements of him were sure of the fact, yet the creature could not be seen. Many times did Gillimal turn and stare into the distance behind them, but to no avail. Whatever it was, kept skilfully out of sight, lurking in the shadows, where it watched with malicious intent.

Gillimal refrained from mentioning this to Jeremy, mindful that the child before him already had enough to carry on his small shoulders. He felt a sense of pride, as a father might, as he watched Jeremy walking steadily beside him, keeping pace with his long stride without a single grumble of complaint. Eringuild had thrown so many challenges in his path and yet Jeremy looked and felt better for it. Despite aching feet and stiffness in his joints, his skin had gained a healthy redness in the cheeks, compared to the paler sickly colour he had been at home. His muscles had tightened due to the immense amount of walking and running he had undertaken, and despite having been in the throes of danger for most of his time in Eringuild, Jeremy felt a true feeling of being alive and sensitive to everything around him.

He had been a shell of himself at home, confined in spirit as well as movement, but he had broken free now, this was the Jeremy he was meant to be.

By the time they reached the giant country though, he was feeling weary. The land was not by any means as dark and dismal as the shadow lands but was in no way welcoming either. You were not encouraged to stay by either its landscape or the thought of its occupants. The land seemed mainly of rock, separated by great crevasses; some foliage could be seen but very little compared to the lush greenness of the central regions.

In the distance, stood the giant mountain, rising upwards from the sea, cold and intimidating, with only the outline of one or two trees framed in its silhouette to offer any comfort. The country gave one the distinct impression they wanted to leave, not least from the prospect of meeting a giant.

Jeremy expressed this worry and Gillimal tried to reassure him.

'Yes, it is true that they are the biggest of any creature you will see here, but not in any way the most dangerous. To begin with, the giant nation is small, drawing strength from their size rather than their numbers. Secondly they do not see well – all the world must seem moving dots to them, so if in doubt, stay still. There is an excellent chance that would save you. Thirdly, as throughout our quest, we are together and nothing will befall you whilst you travel in my care. Now we are in the country,' Gillimal continued, 'it will be harder to find water. The giants use the sea as their source and this is where we too must aim. It will take us closer to the giant's castle than I would have chosen but it is a risk we must take. Once at the shore, our new direction will be plain through the message we receive and we will travel without detection.' And so they walked on, Jeremy watching his surroundings intently and listening for that familiar thunderous tread.

They carried on in this manner, quietly observing their surroundings, whilst their follower continued also, watching their every move. Finally, they came to the foundations of the giant mountain, so vast that Jeremy could not see the summit as he gazed upwards at the enormous structure.

'Do we have to climb that?' he asked Gillimal, his heart truly sinking, for the first time since his journey began.

'No, my friend. There is a valley not far away that will lead us directly to the sea. But beware, as giants do use that way too and so we must be especially on our guard from now on.'

They continued their walk, staying close to the

mountainside, where Gillimal said they would be safest. The valley appeared more like a tunnel, as the sides of the mountains were so high around it. Jeremy walked now with some reticence in his tread; the valley was not pleasant like the one when he arrived in Eringuild. It was cast in shadow and even the mountain itself seemed to leer down at you. Jeremy looked upwards, relieved to still see the sky, although half expecting a giant's head to be staring down from the top of the mountain, grinning at the foes that would now be so easy to catch.

These thoughts occupied Jeremy's mind until a noise broke through and it cheered him greatly. What he could now hear was the sound of the sea, the lapping of the waves along the shore and the occasional crash as they broke amongst the rocks, frothing with foam.

They had reached the sea, or at least almost. Jeremy's heart was gladdened by the thought of the sea at home. Swimming, building sandcastles, and eating delicious ice creams as they melted in the hot sun and dripped down your fingers.

'Finally!' exclaimed Gillimal, who, if truth were told, had also been feeling the strain of the journey. They were now at the end of the valley, a sandy plain before them, intermitted with pieces of rock, jutting upwards through the sand. The great sea was beyond that; so close that Jeremy could smell the salt in the air. Gillimal beckoned his companion towards him and whispered in a soft voice.

'We are closest to our cause, but nearest to danger, my friend,' he said. 'On such an open plain as this, there will be little protection from any that might be watching. We must move swiftly down to the water's edge and read our message with all the speed that is possible. We shall then return here to this point,' and he patted the rock of the mountain besides him. 'Here we can think how best to continue with the safety of the mountain to hide us. Beware of the rock pools though, Jeremy,' he said. 'They are not like the ones you are accustomed to in your own land. Giant pools hold giant things and it would be very unwise to approach them any closer than necessary.'

Jeremy nodded and Gillimal edged out into the open, holding his hoof backwards in a motion for Jeremy to stay still. The Asrah looked carefully around him, sniffing the air and scouring the horizon of the mountain for any danger and when he was satisfied, he flicked his hoof for Jeremy to follow. The two set out briskly for the sea before them, both trying to ignore the sense of dread they felt. Soon the sand became wet underfoot and then water itself was in sight.

'We must move into the water itself,' said Gillimal, 'else the movement of the waves with take the message away with it.'

The two entered the water, paddling at first and then wading, as the level of the water rose up their bodies.

'Quick Jeremy!' Gillimal said, as he looked around once more. 'The bottle – let us read the message.'

Jeremy opened the vial with trembling fingers and the much-needed message appeared:

That which you seek is here with you,
The one who knows it is here too.
Talk with the ones who cannot speak,
But know all and everything that you seek.

'The trees,' said Gillimal. 'The trees must know where the acorn is! Wipe the message, Jeremy, we know our quest!'

And then a terrible thing happened.

As Jeremy bent to erase the message, he felt a shadow cover the entire area around him. He slowly looked back at Gillimal and his face contorted in a look of horror, as he too was fixed in shadow, cast from an enormous figure behind him. Gillimal knew there was no chance of escape and called to Jeremy, 'Stay down, stay down!'

Just as a giant set of fingers clasped Gillimal's body and drew him up into the air. Jeremy flung himself down into the water, submerging all except his head. Gillimal had almost disappeared from sight but Jeremy still heard the words, 'Keep safe and out of sight. Help will come, Jeremy, it will come…' and the last words trailed off as Gillimal was taken away.

*

The Asrah was horizontal in the air, his body swaying with the movement of who carried him, but he could only get a fleeting glimpse of his captor. He struggled but the grip was firm enough to keep him in place.

'Hey!' he bellowed in the loudest voice he could

muster. 'You up there! I am Gillimal of the Asrahs and I command that you release me and return me to the ground!'

The giant then stopped walking and Gillimal found himself being lifted higher and higher until he was level with his captor's face. There, to his surprise, he found he was looking into the face of a male child, with a full grin and freckles, each of giant proportions.

He looked at Gillimal and appeared to chuckle, in a way that suggested he was pleased with himself.

'I caught one!' it boomed. 'I caught one!' He bounced on the spot with excitement.

'Put me down!' Gillimal cried, giddy with the movement.

Suddenly the grip around him tightened and the child said, 'Quiet, bad fishy!' and then lowered Gillimal with the quickness he was raised and put him in the inside of what seemed to be a box.

'You be good,' the giant child said, waggling a finger in mock sternness. He chuckled again and Gillimal felt the box being raised. As it was, the other objects in the box bashed and slid around him: a piece of slimy seaweed and a dead crab, probably fortunate enough to have been found that way. Gillimal could only see the sky as they travelled and thought with despair of Jeremy, he had failed him!

Holding back his head, Gillimal let forth a familiar bellow that loud as it was, was not noticed by the creature that carried him, but it moved on the wind over Eringuild and was heard by some; clear and distinct as a bell.

Gillimal was now feeling the sensation that his carrier was walking up a steep hill. He could no longer hear the splash of the water beneath him and the box had started to tip, sending all the contents crashing into him once again. The climb continued and then Gillimal could no longer see the sky. He could see what looked like rafters far up in the distance above him, and glimpses of stone.

I must be inside a building but it's difficult to tell where, he thought to himself. Suddenly, all movement stopped and the Asrah listened intently for any clues of his surroundings.

Should he have been able to see, he would have witnessed that he was in an immense hall, long and thin with a walkway down the middle. Along the walls at certain points were lamps, lit by unknown means, each radiating a piercing glow.

At the end of the room was a giant throne upon which the giant king sat. The remainder of the giant population were sat around him at long tables; they seemed to be partaking of a meal. The child bounced up towards the king fearlessly, whose face lit in pleasure when he saw him.

'There you are, my son!' he exclaimed in a voice that echoed throughout the room. 'What have you been doing?'

The child looked shyly at the box (which Gillimal saw him peer into) and then back at his father. 'Fishing, Dada – down by the sea.'

'And what did you catch, my son?' the giant asked, continuing a smile that showed great fondness. The child, eager to show his treasures, now delved inside the box with a clumsy hand, grasping first the crab by a claw.

'This!' he exclaimed, waggling the poor creature about as if it were a puppet.

'And?' said the king.

'And this!' said the child, pulling out the piece of seaweed.

'Good catching, my son,' he said. 'But these must have been easy to find, is there anything else?'

The child sensed a slight disappointment in his father's words, although he couldn't, at his young age explain it, and now looked at Gillimal, lifting him out with surprising care.

As he appeared out of the box there was a general gasp from the giants, except the king who instantly burst into great reels of laughter.

'Now, my son,' he said, 'that really is a catch!' And the giants started to laugh in unison.

The child looked puzzled, unsure why they were laughing at his treasure.

'Fancy that!' the king continued. 'An Asrah being caught in the sea, I did not know they could swim!'

Gillimal, at this point, had had quite enough of being suspended in the air and even more so of being sneered at.

'You have no right to have done this!' he bellowed and the room went silent. 'You know the laws as they apply to us all. Let us agree that this has been a mistake and let me on my way.'

'You speak plainly, Asrah,' said the king, 'but you

needn't preach to me about the laws, I know them well. But have you not heard?' the king continued in mock surprise, 'the acorn has been stolen and the laws that we are bound to are wearing thin. Without the symbol of peace in our midst, what governs any of us?'

And then his face became hard and his smile quickly disappeared.

'Too long have the Asrahs walked freely across our lands, the lands we were banished to, in the furthest part of Eringuild. We have always been overlooked, when all the good things were handed out. And yet, how the situation has changed! I have you here, in my country, surrounded by my men and in the presence of my child and you think that I should just let you go? Well no,' he sneered, 'I will not! You have travelled far to our lands and it would be rude for us to send you away so soon. So you shall stay. Take him to the dungeons.'

A giant guard moved towards the Asrah and the child who clasped him.

'No Dada, no!' screamed the child, beginning a giant tantrum. 'He is mine, Dada. I found him and I want him. No, no!' He smacked at the guard with his free hand, pulling Gillimal away out of his grasp.

'Kinismear, stop it!' his father commanded. 'Dada knows best.' He signalled for the guard to seize Gillimal.

'No!' the child called stubbornly, and dodging the guard with some skill, ran towards his father and placed a loving hand on his knee, a giant tear splashing from his eye onto Gillimal like a bucket of salty water.

'Please, Dada!' the child implored, and looked lovingly at his father. The king looked down at his son, the only one that he really cared for, and his hard heart softened at the sight of the child so puzzled by adult events.

'Listen Kinismear,' the giant king said, lifting the child onto his lap. 'Dada is going to put him somewhere safe so you can keep him. If not, he might run away. Will you give him to Dada, Kinismear?'

The child faltered for a second before placing the Asrah gently in his father's outstretched hand.

'Good boy,' the king said, and patted his head with his free hand. He motioned for the guard to come forward.

'Dada,' said the child suddenly, grasping his father's tunic. 'Don't hurt him, he mine!'

The king nodded.

'No harm shall befall him, Kinismear. I promise.' Gillimal saw him held in his father's arms, as he was carried away.

15

A Surprise Meeting

This time Gillimal at least had the advantage of seeing where he was going. Previously they had been travelling up, to the giant halls, which were built upon the mountain itself making them taller still. But now, he could see that they were heading down, out of the throne room and deeper downwards so that soon, as they passed through doors and corridors, the walls became of earth and not rock.

We must now be inside the mountain, he thought. Suddenly his carrier stopped and before them, as much as Gillimal could see, was a large cavern, formed by digging into the rock, with bars across it to hold prisoners within.

'Guest quarters,' laughed the guard with surprising wit, and opened a small section of the bars in front of him, which turned out to be the door, and pushed Gillimal roughly inside. He locked it again, putting the key in a fold of his garment. Gillimal waited until the great form before him had disappeared from sight and then went towards the bars. Being designed to imprison larger enemies from times long ago, the bars were quite well spread and Gillimal remembered the time centuries ago that the giants were of a thriving population, immense and fearsome but divided as they warred against each other.

There had always been a settlement in the castle itself but until lately there had always been others to fight for it too. But now the population was diminished, broken down through the events of the past and these bars were merely a symbol of something that once had been but now was no more.

Gillimal attempted to squeeze his body through the gap, which he could do, except for his fine antlers. They grew at such angles that no matter which way he turned, they could not pass through with the rest of him. He tried in vain but eventually gave up, anxious not to be caught in the action. He now inspected the walls, running his hooves along them and looking intently. Suddenly his hoof jumped up like it had bumped into something obstructing its path. It was difficult to see in the dimming light but Gillimal smiled when he recognised what it was.

A tree root! To think of the leaves so far above on the summit of the mountain. This was good news indeed!

Gillimal knelt by the root, preparing to talk with the tree. It was a delicate art, known only by a few in Eringuild now. First, he had to clear his mind of all other things. He closed his eyes and listened. He heard nothing and behind his closed eyelids, a heavy blackness began to form and the Asrah slipped into the necessary state, raising only his hooves to the tree itself, where they made a flash of light against the bark. They were now as one and the tree felt it too. It was unused to being called, as it hardly ever occurred anymore, and sensing with its roots, quickly learnt who was calling.

Trees as we know, cannot speak or smile or laugh; yet this one would have done all three if it could. It remembered Gillimal and was tired of the loneliness of its position in the giant world. So now, it sent its message down the tree from the leaves right to the roots and when they reached Gillimal, a picture formed in front of his eyes. He saw the giant and shadow king meeting on the mountainside and a golden shape between them. The acorn! He saw also the shadow king, stealing a ruby, prising it off with his bare hand and clutching it to him. Then the picture changed and this was a symbol of a new day, where the giant king returned to the spot where he had stood with the shadow king and this time, dug up the acorn and took it away with him. What Gillimal saw next was as if he were looking straight upwards to where the tree broke from the ground, so that he could see the sky and then he shuddered, as the image of the giant king's looming face blotted it out, as he looked down towards him and put a golden item down into the earth, before covering it up and then all was black again.

Gillimal's eyes then shot open and he rested his head against the root, which was an age-old symbol of gratitude, before he rolled over to think.

The giant king had buried the acorn in the boughs

of this tree. Only the earth now directly above was between him and it. Yet this revelation was clouded by a sense of something else. He was a prisoner and Jeremy was somewhere out in the giant country alone. He hoped that his call had been answered and that help was on its way to his young friend.

*

Whilst Gillimal thought helplessly in the giant's castle, Jeremy was also feeling rather lost himself. Gillimal had been his guide and friend for so long, he did not know what to do without him. But he remembered what Gillimal had shouted to him and trusted that help would be coming soon. Jeremy headed back across the beach away from the water and the giant pools, where many monsters lurked as shadows beneath the surface, and headed towards the protection of the mountains. Perhaps, if he could just stay out of sight, he would be all right.

What he didn't know was that he was still being watched and had been since he left Glubin Town. The servant of the black sun was always hidden from view, but had never let the small boy out of his sight for a moment. He had witnessed the capture of Gillimal and was now watching Jeremy approach towards him, completely unaware of the danger. *How easy it would be*, the creature thought, *to just do away with him now. He is all alone and without help, who then would take the acorn back to Tayrah? All their plans would be laid to waste.* He was so taken with this idea that his fingers began to twitch, ready for their evil purpose.

But then, continued the creature to itself, *if I follow him still, I will find the acorn and without that Asrah to protect him, I can easily take it for myself and his life too if I wish it.*

These were the thoughts that Jeremy was so unaware of, as he walked briskly back to the base of the mountains and the valley, down which he had just travelled with Gillimal. As he headed back, he thought he must be dreaming, as there, approaching him steadily, was Gillimal, as if he had never been away.

'Gillimal!' Jeremy exclaimed, and ran towards him. But the creature put its hoof to his lips and shuffled Jeremy out of the open and back to the mountainside.

'You must be Jeremy,' he whispered.

'Yes,' said Jeremy slowly, beginning to realise what was happening.

'My name is Aritide,' the Asrah continued. 'Gillimal called us and I have brought the Asrah nation to help you.'

'Nation?' said Jeremy, puzzled. 'But I can only see you!'

The Asrah smiled and pointed upwards with his hoof.

There, before Jeremy's eyes, the horizon moved in a single brown mass, as hundreds of Asrahs came into sight and marched towards him down the mountainside, all armed and ready for battle. They clustered behind Aritide and those at the front, bowed their great heads slightly to Jeremy, as a mark of respect.

'You really are an army!' Jeremy exclaimed. 'But what are you going to do?'

'Rescue Gillimal to begin with,' said Aritide. 'He has been taken by the giants, has he not?' Jeremy nodded. 'And then he will direct us from there. Stay close, Jeremy,' the Asrah smiled. 'Although when you travel with the Asrah army, there is very little that can harm you! Let us go to Gillimal. He has been prisoner long enough.'

Aritide signalled onwards and the Asrahs began to move. What a glorious sight they looked, and with a little boy marching so bravely alongside them.

*

Gillimal continued to think in his cavern prison, as there was not much else he could do. *There have been many surprises today*, he thought. *First to be captured by a child, albeit a giant one, and then to be so misguided about the giants themselves! I fear that they have been grossly underestimated over the years. They showed surprising intelligence before me and no fear of consequences.*

For all the years I have known the giant population, why have I never seen this before? I am at fault in more than one way today. What else will be sent to test me?

As if in answer, he was suddenly aware of a noise on the far side of the cavern and sprang to his feet in readiness.

'Who is there?' he demanded, but was met only by silence. 'Do not make me ask again,' he continued and heard a slow shuffle as a creature approached. As it came into what light there was, the Asrah witnessed a hooded figure, bent over as if threatened, making him small in appearance. Gillimal himself was unsure what creature this was.

'Show yourself,' he said. 'Who are you?'

As it stepped forward into the light, he brought up his hands and removed his hood and Gillimal gasped in surprise for there before him, altered only by the presence of a bushy brown beard on his face, was Henry Applegate.

'Henry, it's you!' the Asrah exclaimed joyfully, more for Jeremy's sake than for his own. 'This is where you have been!'

Henry frowned and squinted at Gillimal.

'Time in this light means I cannot see you well, stranger. Who are you and how do know my name?'

'I have known you since you came to this land,' Gillimal said. 'I watched you enter, leave, and return many times afterwards.'

Henry still looked puzzled and Gillimal continued: 'I can see this is a lot for you to understand and that you don't really trust me. What if I were to tell you that at this very moment, your son is here too?'

Henry raised his face, showing both worry and happiness in his expression.

'Jeremy is here?' he exclaimed. 'It cannot be true!'

'It is most certainly,' said Gillimal. 'Until I became prisoner here, he was my own travelling companion, safe and well. Only bad luck has parted us. But,' he said sympathetically, 'I can see that you have been no stranger to bad luck yourself. How did you come to be in the land of the giants?'

Henry hobbled forwards towards the bars, as if his body were stiff and tired, and sat on the ground opposite Gillimal, who did the same.

'As you say,' Henry began, 'I entered Eringuild on many occasions, and was eager to explore the new world. I knew it was dangerous, and every time I returned home, I promised myself that was the last time. But it never was. Eringuild cast a spell of some sort over me; something kept calling me back.

'I had until then been very wary in my travels across the country, not knowing the creatures that lived there. But everywhere I visited, I sketched in my journal, always trying to learn more. I had spent the majority of my time around the marshlands and the central regions but wanted to see what else I could discover. One day, I set off across the countryside heading south, but I wandered too far into the giant realms, where I was taken as a prisoner. At first, I thought they were just fearsome beasts, who captured anyone they could, but later realised their true intentions, and that they had a dark purpose in mind for me. Whilst imprisoned, I listened carefully to what the giants were saying at every chance I had. Slowly but surely I pieced together the story of the acorn and its planned robbery. On one occasion, I heard the giant talking to somebody, but I could not see who. They spoke in low whispers and discussed the taking of the acorn from the castle of Tayrah. It was then that my dreaded purpose came to light. The giant king was not going to steal it himself but send me in his place!

'Of course I refused at once but the king gave me his solemn word, that I would be released from their lands if my quest were successful. Since my forced stay in Eringuild, all I had thought of was returning home to my wife and Jeremy, who I knew, with great sadness, would have thought I had deserted them. For this reason alone, I agreed to the mission and set out across the lands to Tayrah. The king had given me instructions on what I was to do there and had informed me that I was to meet somebody at first dark. Getting into the castle was surprisingly easy. I later found out that Eringuild was under the impression that the acorn was guarded by a magic spell, cast by the wizard who made it. As it turned out, it was only this myth that protected it.

'There was no such spell in place and I easily lifted the acorn from its holder in the main room of the castle. By this time, it had grown dark and whilst I was there, I had the sense I was being watched. It was then that out of the shadows, appeared a creature I had never seen before. Cloaked and hidden from view, with only a dark hole in the cloth, where its face should have been. This of course I know now, was the shadow king, but he spoke very little, merely informing me that he was to travel back with me to the giant country to see the hiding of the acorn for himself. I could do nothing; this was obviously the way it was going to be, although the creature repulsed me in every possible way. It was then, a most peculiar thing happened. In the candlelight of the room, my shadow became visible and without any further words, the king glided over to it, disappearing at once. At first, I was not sure what had happened but then realised that he was within my shadow, hidden from view but still very much there! I tucked the acorn into my garments and set off back to the giant kingdom, disgusted that this creature was coming with me in such a way.

'As we travelled, the sun began to rise but into a sky filled with morning fog, so that it looked pale, as it tried its best to shine through. I shivered, more with the thought of what I had done than with the cold of morning, but returned to my place of capture. I now understood the full meaning of the acorn and the twin rubies surrounding it.

'It was bad enough that the acorn was taken to them, but I realised I could take a ruby away from them quite easily and it would be unlikely that they would see. With the shadow king, still in my shadow, I carefully removed a ruby from its shell of gold and put it in my pocket. As I reached the giant kingdom, I was most glad that I did, as the giant king had no intention of keeping his promise to me and instead locked me in this very cavern in which we now sit, only moments after my passenger rose from my shadow and jumped into the king's! Of course I still had the ruby and I knew that I had to get it far away from the giant kingdom for it to be safe. I know now that I perhaps made things more difficult by separating them, but I thought I was doing the right thing at the time. I was determined not to let them find it, so I waited for my chance to escape. I got as far as Glubin Town by the early hours one morning. When they caught up with me, I was by the water's edge and meant to bury the thing to come back later but instead, in my haste, it dropped from my fingers and sank into the water. It was then that the giant king caught me and returned me to their kingdom as a prisoner in his pocket. He had no intention of letting me go, as he knew it was against the laws of Eringuild to have kept me prisoner in the first place.

'They have watched me most carefully since my return and keep me down here, under the mountain where there is less chance of my escape. I do not know what happened to the acorn after I brought it here, as I was not there to see.'

'I can continue for you,' Gillimal joined in. 'The second ruby was stolen by the shadow king, without the knowledge of the giants, not long after its burial. It was then taken back to his own lands, when he left under the protection of night, but that ruby is now with Jeremy. The other that you spoke of is too. But that's a tale for another time.'

'So Jeremy has both rubies?' Henry questioned, feeling a sense of pride towards his son.

Gillimal nodded. 'But now we must find him to finish our quest. We are running very short of time in this matter,' he said gravely.

'We must leave here as soon as possible to tell him what we now know, but it won't be easy. We must think of a plan!

The pair continued to talk as the bright sun of Eringuild prepared to set for the night ahead.

*

In the rooms above them, the giant king was consulting with his people.

'Is the prisoner kept?' he questioned his guard.

'Yes my lord, he cannot escape.'

'Good, and that is the way it must remain,' said the king. 'I have some business to attend to which will take me out to the mountain. Guard our prisoner well and keep watch for any other unwelcome visitors coming our way. If they do, let them witness how fearsome our nation really is.'

He turned to leave.

'And,' he continued, suddenly remembering a more important instruction.

'Yes, my liege?' said the guard.

'Do not let Kinismear follow me today,' said the king, lowering his voice as he looked over to his throne, where the child was playing.

'Keep him here within the walls and keep him safe above all things.'

The guard merely nodded in compliance, as the king strode down the hall and away on his business.

16

Attack of the Asrahs

As the giant king left the castle that evening, little did he know of the attack that was shortly to follow. The Asrah nation were already there and watching; flat against the ground with only their antlers seen against the outline of the mountain.

'There goes the king,' said Aritide. 'We must attack soon before he returns.'

Facing his followers, he continued.

'You all know what we must do. Find Gillimal and free him, whilst holding off the giants as well as we can.'

The Asrahs nodded together, creating a moving brown mass of heads and antlers. Signalling to a section of the crowd to his left, they began to move out, when Aritide raised his hoof again to stop, as something unexpected had happened. Leaving the castle was the giant child Kinismear, having deceived his watcher and snuck out of the castle, in search of his father.

'Asrahs, halt!' ordered Aritide. 'What luck! The giant child is approaching, I now see a way to save Gillimal without the fight we had intended.'

He whispered his new plans to a general by his shoulder.

Poor Kinismear was completely unaware of the attack until the very last moment, when hundreds of Asrahs broke from the hill, charging down towards him. Giant child he was, but no match for the army before him and he stood in childlike wonder, as they came closer and closer.

But despite his size, he was still a child and now reacted in fear, trying to run back to the safety of the castle. But alas, he slipped and fell to the sand. The Asrahs seized their chance and were upon him, covering his body like a brown carpet, and it was not long before the child was completely held down, unable to move.

Aritide climbed onto his body and stood at the top of his chest, looking down into the huge but frightened face before him.

'It is all right, child,' he said in a loud but kind voice. 'No one is going to hurt you. But we do need to see your father. Call him for us.'

The child was more relaxed by the gentle tone of voice, but still called loudly for his father to save him, but of course, he was not there to hear. Instead came the guard, whose face dropped in horror as he saw what had become of Kinismear. Aritide called to him from their position and said, 'Where is your king? We wish to speak with him.'

'He is away on business,' the giant called back. 'Release his son at once or prepare for the consequences.'

'I cannot do that,' said Aritide, 'at least not at the moment. I have a prisoner and so do you. Release Gillimal to us and we'll return the child to you.'

The giant hesitated and Aritide continued,

'Or else we shall wait and see what your king makes of this and what has befallen his son whilst in your care.'

The giant turned swiftly and disappeared into the castle.

'No tricks now,' Aritide called after him. 'We shall wait here.'

Kinismear was sobbing softly to himself and Jeremy felt sorry for one much like himself, although so much bigger in size. Kinismear's hand and huge fingers lay close to him, flexing in his current distress. One of the fingers was roughly Jeremy's size and he hugged it like it was a person. Kinismear felt the squeeze and turned his head to see the cause. He smiled shyly in surprise when he saw the little boy and Jeremy smiled back.

'There, there,' he said, patting the finger before him. 'It will all be all right. There is nothing for you to be worried about.'

Suddenly giant footsteps could again be heard and the ground began to shake. The giant returned with two figures walking behind him. Jeremy stared in disbelief as they approached and he recognised his old friend Gillimal and by his side, his father, Henry Applegate!

'Daddy!' he called excitedly. 'Daddy! Daddy!'

And he ran across the sand, slipping and stumbling towards his father.

Henry heard the familiar call and squinted into the distance to see the figure of Jeremy approaching towards him. He too began to run and the two figures met amongst the sand, hugging each other tightly as Gillimal looked on and smiled. Something lost had now been found.

'Now,' called the giant, 'give Kinismear back to us. Remember your bargain.'

'Indeed I do,' replied the Asrah. 'But how can I be sure that you will not attack us as soon as the child is returned?'

For that thought had indeed been running through the giant's vengeful mind.

'You can't,' he sneered. 'What will be, will be.'

'That's not good enough,' said the Asrah. 'We will keep Kinismear until you promise not to harm us.'

The giant lunged forward, just as the voice of the king could suddenly be heard on the mountainside. He had returned unexpectedly, only to see his child, captured by the enemy and was lost in his sadness.

'Kinismear!' he called in despair.

Kinismear, hearing his father, raised his head to call, 'Dada, Dada!'

The giant king stormed down into the valley,

stopping before the Asrah army.

'What is the meaning of this?' he boomed.

'Ah, King,' said Gillimal, 'we are just negotiating our terms. Kinismear will not be harmed on one condition.'

'Speak,' said the giant, 'and give my child back to me.'

'Certainly,' replied Gillimal. 'We need only your word that neither you nor any of your kind will hurt us whilst we remain in your land. Promise us this and Kinismear is safe.'

The giant normally would have lied through his teeth to outwit any enemy but his heart was flooded with worry for Kinismear, and when he saw his son's gentle eyes looking upon him, he realised for the first time in his life, the importance of giving his word and meaning it.

What has any of this been worth? he now thought. *The acorn, the upcoming war, for what did any of it matter without Kinismear?*

Calling to him, he said, 'You are all that is good in me, my son. And I promise not to hurt the Asrahs, for you. Come to me,' and he opened his arms towards him.

Gillimal nodded and the moving mass of Asrahs leapt off Kinismear, allowing him to stand and run to his father, thundering across the sand. When the king was holding his child in his arms, he called back, 'Do here what you will. The giant nation will not stop you. I have with me now, all that I care about.'

And he turned and walked towards the castle, signalling for the guard to go back inside.

17

The End of the Shadow King

Under the cover of night, the shadow king had travelled at fastest speed, whispering evils into the ear of the shadow horse to make it run with fear and dread. It frothed around its mouth, its mane matted to its black body, and its eyes were wide with fright. They had travelled most of the length of Eringuild in a few hours and the giant's mountain was now in sight in the distance. The horse kept its pace as they galloped up the mountainside but soon the land became rocky and of such a gradient it could not climb any further. The shadow king dismounted, squinting in the twilight, recognising the summit from his last visit. With all the speed he could muster, he continued up the mountainside, groaning with the strain it put upon his limbs. Finally, he reached the summit and searched for that place which marked the acorn was beneath. He found it, a tall tree, reaching high into the night sky, having grown throughout many moons of Eringuild. The king dropped to his knees and began to claw at the soft earth surrounding the tree. Suddenly there was a thundering in the air and the ground shook as if with fear. A giant was approaching, the king of the giants himself, and his face was of thunder too.

The shadow king had nowhere to hide and only his cunning now to protect him.

'It is plain you see me as a fool!' the giant king bellowed. 'Did you think you could enter my land, without my knowing, and steal the acorn from me?'

'You mistake me,' said the shadow king. 'Have you not heard that the enemy forces are upon us? They only need the acorn to thwart our plans for power. It must be moved to safety and a new location but I was acting for both of us! Is our allegiance not worth the belief in that?'

'I don't know what your allegiance is worth at all!' the giant sniggered. 'You lie with the ease of a demon, as even now you think you can overcome me with your words of poison, but you are the fool if you believe it! Do you imagine that I ever trusted you and your kind? You who live in darkness, and your souls are dark too? Before I had even realised you had stolen a ruby and taken it in secret back to your land, I had already removed the acorn from its hiding place, realising I could only trust in my own people and not the monsters you call yours!'

The shadow king had now taken enough of the insults from this speech and his civil tone faltered with all the malice of his anger pushing through.

'Fool!' he cried to the giant king. 'You're fool

indeed! What do you think it matters, if you have the acorn? Without the rubies it is worthless and wherever its location may be, without them, Eringuild will still fall. My great nation will rise to power as the leaders of the darkness. You, for all your height will bow to me, along with all the other nations of this land. Even one with such limited intelligence as you, must recognise this truth as it stares at you!'

But in his keenness to mock, the shadow king had made a fatal error. Eringuild had been growing steadily lighter and now the break of dawn was slowly spreading over the land. The shadow king turned in horror to witness that which he was forbidden to see. The giant king smiled a cruel smile.

'Fool, am I?' he cried. 'Who is the fool now caught in the sun, without the darkness to save him?'

The shadow king's body started to heave and he dropped to the ground. As the light met his body, he began to glow. It could be seen under his robes and it spread over him like a golden butter. If he could just make it to the giant's shadow! He crawled towards it with all the strength he had left but alas, for him it was too late. With one mighty step backwards, he was without hope again and fell once more to the ground, now glowing from every bone in his body.

As the giant looked on, the shadow king began to dissolve in the light, pieces of his bony exterior floating up into the air like fragments from a bonfire. All that was left were his bones, still inside his robes, and the giant picked them up in one enormous hand and threw them down into the valley below, golden pieces glittering with them. As the sun reached its full glory that morning, there ended the life of the shadow king.

18

The Final Battle

Meanwhile back in the valley, Gillimal and Aritide were deep in conversation.

'The giants may now not be a threat to us,' Aritide said wisely, 'but the black sun still remains our greatest enemy. We must not let this victory blur our vision, the black sun is still ever dangerous and will not accept defeat so lightly. It will fight us with all it has and we must be ready for its final attack.

'The Asrahs stand with you, Gillimal,' he continued. 'If they fight with full force, then so shall we and remain here until the task is complete.'

'You are wise as you are brave,' Gillimal replied, 'but this is a time of great danger and each Asrah must make their own decision.'

In answer, the Asrah nation bellowed in unison, a mighty noise which echoed throughout the valley.

'All great things come at much cost,' said Aritide, 'and their choice appears to be made.'

As if in answer, suddenly a great noise could be heard in the sky and the companions turned to see the black sun, shaking as if in anger. Its surface appeared to be bubbling, as if being moved from the inside and in the blink of an eye, it burst out, spraying the air with black shapes that blotted out the sky, as they fell to the earth.

'So it is time,' Aritide said bravely. 'Asrahs, ready!' Turning to Gillimal, he said: 'Run, my friend. Do not stop until the acorn is found!'

Gillimal nodded and calling to Jeremy, began to run towards the mountain.

From the opposite direction, a sea of black shapes was heading towards the Asrahs, moving in mass like a heavy black cloud. At first, they drifted over the ground moving as one, and then as they came into view, showed themselves to be all kinds of shapes and sizes, twisted and contorted and all darkest black. Some had horns, some fangs, and some claws. None of them were the same as his neighbour, for they were the army of the black sun, created for the single purpose of fighting good; given physical form by its power and filled with the thoughts of its black mind.

The Asrahs stood their ground. Many were carrying long sticks and they angled them towards their enemies.

For a split second there seemed to be silence, and then the air was filled with the sound of battle as the two sides collided and began to fight. The enemy were hungry for war and made a variety of snarls and growls and snapping noises, where the Asrahs were silent, warriors of old, fighting with grace and strength but with deadly purpose. As they struck their enemy, their bodies turned to the black dust from where they came and the numbers began to lessen. The black sun too appeared to shrink in size as its army did, appearing less daunting in the sky.

Gillimal and Jeremy by now had almost reached the tree. Gillimal recognised it as soon as he saw it.

'This is it, Jeremy,' he said. 'This is the place. Quickly, we must dig.' And he pointed with his hoof to the soft earth around the roots of the great tree.

As they both clawed the ground in search of the precious acorn, their follower had silently appeared from the shadows, where he had, until now, been watching. Gillimal's fur bristled as he felt the presence and he smelt that all too familiar smell of decay. He knew before he looked, who stood before him, and was prepared for a battle of his own.

'Your work in this tale is done,' said Gillimal. 'Return to your master whilst it still knows what power is.'

The creature grinned, showing two rows of rotten teeth and a black tongue between them. 'Fool!' he rasped. 'Even after all your years in Eringuild, you still do not recognise your rightful master.'

'The Asrahs have no master,' said Gillimal bravely. 'We serve only this country.'

'Look round at your beloved country, Asrah,' sneered the enemy, 'for in a few moments, it will belong to us.'

At this point, he ran forward, jumping at Gillimal, who pulled him to the floor as the two rolled and tussled, each fighting the strength of the other. Gillimal kicked with his colossal legs and hooves, whilst the other tried to restrain him with punching blows. Jeremy looked on, helpless, until with the force of their movement, Tirimae's bag opened and an unknown object fell out. It was a petal and suddenly Jeremy could hear the warlock speak, as if he was whispering in his ear, beside him.

'This is the most precious item of all. It recognises your wishes and will turn into anything to help you. Be strong Jeremy, you know in your heart what to do.'

Jeremy raised his head to see the creature on top of Gillimal, pinning him to the ground.

'This is your end,' he hissed down at Gillimal, who could only squirm, as his opponent prepared to deliver the final blow.

Jeremy froze in horror, watching the scene before him. Moments from his memory came flooding into his mind, how helpless he had been at home, surrounded by loneliness and unable to find the truth. He had only discovered his own importance since coming to Eringuild and as much of a fairy tale as it all seemed to him, this was real.

As he looked at his friend before him, Jeremy felt helpless no more. It was up to him to save Gillimal now and grasping the petal in his hand, he closed his eyes and wished for the first thing he thought could help. The enemy saw none of this as Jeremy was behind him, until a strange sensation made him loosen his grip. His entire body was now tingling in an unpleasant way, flickers of feelings running up and down his body like a tiny army. He let go of Gillimal and staggered back, staring down at one of his hands. It was stiffening before him and try as he might, he was now struggling to move it. The fingers contorted in a slow motion before stopping altogether. His skin was also changing colour to a pale grey and the rest of the body was beginning to follow. He dropped to his knees, which turned out to be his last movement in Eringuild, and Gillimal watched in wonder as the figure before him turned to stone, sat upon his knees with his head bowed, looking in horror at his hands before him.

For Jeremy had wished for Gillimal's attacker to be unable to move and the petal had heard. He now stepped cautiously towards the statue, peering at the face that was still, even now, frightening to behold. As he reached out a hand gingerly, his fingers met only the coldness of stone and then the figure began to crack.

Slowly at first, cracks rising upwards from the floor and joining together, as they travelled across the limbs until finally crumbling into black dust, which was caught in the breeze and blown gently down the mountainside into the valley below. The black sun, as if witnessing this, groaned in the sky and shrunk further in size. Both sides below saw this and it filled the Asrahs with hope and the black army with dread. Most of the enemy had now been dispatched or were fleeing at their shrinking sun. Those remaining now turned their heads in horror up to the horizon of the mountain, where two figures were standing side by side, Gillimal bellowing to his nation below and

Jeremy shouting in childlike excitement, clutching tightly above his head, a shape that flashed in the sunlight.

The golden acorn had at last been found!

From the top of the mountain, the companions looked down to see the faithful Asrahs holding their position and the last of the black sun's army, scattering in terror to the winds.

19

To Tayrah

Jeremy could not believe that he held the golden acorn in his hands, his quest almost complete. And yet, the biggest challenge of all remained. To return the acorn to its rightful place in Tayrah castle with so little time left before the black sun claimed its endless power. The sky was already darkening around them, and not with the coming of night. The black sun loomed up in the sky before them, smaller but somehow more terrifying than ever before. It would now begin its descent and should it manage to set upon the horizon, everlasting darkness would follow. Jeremy was gazing around in despair, wondering how he was ever going to make it back to the central states, when he heard a soft plodding behind him. Turning to see, there came the shadow king's horse, left now without a rider. Following the events of the night before, he was now aimlessly wandering the hills.

'There,' said Jeremy, looking at the horse. 'That's our way. I shall ride that horse to Tayrah.'

'It is a brave idea,' said Gillimal, 'but that is a shadow horse and it is well known that they are not rideable by any except their masters.'

Jeremy looked at the creature before him, its black mane rippled across his shoulder blades in soft curls. He took a step towards the horse and it stood and watched him.

Jeremy moved closer with his outstretched hand trembling slightly and the horse sniffed his fingers, gently brushing the skin with his nose.

In truth, the horse did not know what this creature was before him, although it knew it was not a dweller. Needing further reassurance, Jeremy slowly raised his hand so that his fingertips were brushing the cheek of the horse. It was completely surprised by any display of gentleness and stood spellbound as Jeremy began to stroke its face. Both shared a new understanding with the other and Jeremy knew this horse could be ridden. In a smooth motion, he pulled himself up into the saddle, showing a great confidence for one who had never ridden before. He tucked the acorn under his arm and prepared to depart. As he turned the horse, he felt something catch his ankle and he turned to see his father looking up at him imploringly.

'Jeremy,' he said, 'I cannot let you do this. Anything could happen and I won't lose you again!'

Jeremy looked back at him and said gently, 'You must trust me, Daddy, like I trust you. If I don't do this, Eringuild will be destroyed forever and coming here to help will have been for nothing!'

Henry slowly removed his hand from Jeremy's ankle and looking up at the little boy, realised how much he had changed. He stood back as if in agreement and Gillimal gave only a reassuring nod before watching as the travellers became smaller and smaller and finally disappeared over the horizon.

Jeremy and the horse continued across Eringuild, galloping at full speed. The horse seemed to sense the importance of their journey and Jeremy gripped tightly to the reins, as it appeared to go even faster. As he glanced upwards, the menacing form of the black sun seemed to sneer down at the world below.

Eringuild was only a blur as they travelled and Jeremy lost all sense of time. Strangely the horse seemed to know exactly where it was going, as many strange things to us are natural in Eringuild, and at last the outline of Tayrah could be seen in the distance.

Jeremy patted the horse reassuringly, feeling a sense of hope that they were not too late. The horse galloped over the drawbridge and into the courtyard, where Jeremy alighted and looked in awe at his surroundings. It was the biggest castle he had ever seen, with sloping stone walls and towers of varying heights, all pointing their spiky tops far into the sky. His gazing was interrupted by the shadow that came upon him, as the black sun moved over Tayrah. It had been weakened by the loss of the battle but only the replacing of the acorn in Tayrah could destroy it completely. This knowledge somehow seeped into Jeremy's mind, and he was shunted into action by an invisible force. He lurched forward, heading for a spiral staircase that led to an entrance in the castle's huge wall. The door was heavy but not locked and

Jeremy pushed with all his might to enter, making only a small crack, through which he could slip.

On the other side was a hallway, long and thin with candles lit in holders down the walls and Jeremy continued to run, his feet slapping the cold stone. At the end of this, was an enormous room, obviously a throne room as there stood, at the far end, a large throne, stately and grand with a smaller one by its side. Along the walls sitting in pew-like benches were stone figures, bowed with their heads in their hands. In the very middle of the room was a case of glass, built upon a pillar of stone, and there inside the case was an empty velvet cushion, the same colour as the rubies in his pocket. This was surely where the acorn was to rest again!

Jeremy carefully removed the glass lid and taking the rubies from his pocket, pressed them back into their places on the acorn. A sudden electric flash went through his body and he slowly and steadily placed the acorn back on the cushion, closing his eyes to wait for a sign.

Nothing! Nothing happened – the acorn sat on its cushion, as if it had never been moved, and there was for a moment not the smallest sound.

Then suddenly from the sky behind the great windows, came a noise, half groan and half rumble, and the looser items of the room began to move around him, as the tremble spread. Jeremy ran to the window and looking at the black sun, realised that was where the noise was coming from. It was shaking in the sky, slowly at first and then more violently, getting louder and louder, until Jeremy was forced to cover his ears from the din. Then in one glorious moment, the black sun exploded into pieces, its fragments filling the sky and creating a black dust that sunk through the air to the ground below. As it touched the earth, it disappeared, as if it had never been.

Although he was completely alone, Jeremy jumped into the air, punching his fist into the sky in triumph and celebrating the victory that so many others would be sharing.

All across Eringuild the news was spreading. It reached the farthest corners of the land, passing over the marshlands where the Glubins danced and frolicked with glee as Stubb cried out, 'Dem boy, dem boy!' Magdela rose from her watery home and smiled as Glubins dived into the water around her. Even Tirimae in his mountain home rose up the earthy steps to the world above and could be heard exclaiming his joy from the mountain top, his silhouette dark against the sky. Although this news also brought a sense of horror to some, as the shadow dwellers, kingless and alone, cowered in the memory of their defeat. The giants swore their new allegiance to the acorn, a promise that would now bind them throughout time.

Back in the giant lands, the victors of the battle saw it too, as the black cloud of dust darkened the sky and all cheered and celebrated, embracing each other in their victory.

Gillimal, quiet in his happiness, looked only to the horizon and sent across the plains of the world, a silent message that travelled directly to Jeremy's mind as he heard the words, 'Well done, my friend. A thousand times well done!'

20

A Word from the Wizard

Jeremy stood smiling in the castle of Tayrah, when he heard another noise behind him. It was indeed strange, as it sounded like the shifting of stone. For one awful moment, he believed that the castle was going to collapse upon him but when looking around in alarm, realised that the noise was coming from the stone figures, sitting at their benches. They were moving, as their heads were not now bowed in their hands but raised to look straight ahead, with a smile upon their stone lips and their eyes again fixed upon the acorn. Jeremy sighed in relief and then screamed in fright, as the farthest statue from him, winked its stony eye! Jeremy jumped backwards in surprise and looked on in confusion, as the statue started to shake its shoulders, as if it was having some great laugh. As he watched, the stone exterior began to change until there in front of him was a real man, still chuckling at his own joke.

'Oh, I'm sorry Jeremy!' he said. 'I don't see many people and I can never resist that joke, you should have seen yourself, my boy!' Jeremy continued to stare in amazement, as the man jumped up and exclaimed, 'Oh, where are my manners? I have not introduced myself. I am Demasdia, better known as the wizard!'

'You made the acorn,' Jeremy whispered, when he finally found his voice.

'Indeed I did, my boy, as I did this castle. And you have saved it, Jeremy. The acorn is returned and peace shall be again in Eringuild.'

'But I don't understand,' Jeremy said. 'You were here? Have you always been here?'

'Mostly,' said the wizard. 'I like to travel around from time to time but yes, Tayrah is really my home.'

'So…' Jeremy said thoughtfully, 'you have seen it all. Why didn't you help?'

'I wish I could have done, Jeremy,' said the wizard gravely. 'I really do. But I made those rules; I had no more right to break them than anyone else. Peace had to be restored naturally. There is a plan for everything, you know. Your father's coming here was a plan, your following him was a plan, and everything that happened from there and is still happening now is part of a plan. That is the same in all worlds, you know! Everything happens for a reason.'

Jeremy began to understand and nodded his head.

'But,' said the wizard, 'I do think that an actual spell is now needed to protect the acorn against this happening again. I shall see to that presently. But now, to important matters,' he said kindly. 'Do you care for tea?'

*

Jeremy and the wizard sat with tea and cake produced by magic and talked for many hours as the one true sun now shone unchallenged in the vastness of the sky.

'Now,' said the wizard, rising and brushing crumbs of cake from his robe, 'the time has come. You must return to the others and finish your journey. The quest has been completed but your story here must also come to an end.'

Jeremy thought upon this with some sadness, as he realised it would soon be time to leave Eringuild and return to his own world.

'Can I ask you a question?' he said.

'You could indeed,' replied the wizard, 'but it would be needless, as I already know what you are thinking. One never really knows what the future holds, Jeremy, but I would be much surprised if you didn't come back to us one day. You are connected to us now and the call can travel both ways, you know. If help is ever needed, you are and will remain the saviour of Eringuild and you will always hear our call. Now, back to your friends I think!' said the wizard, wiggling his fingers in preparation for another spell.

'Let us walk down to your fine horse,' said the wizard, and it was not long again before Jeremy was upon the saddle.

'You must think carefully where you want to go, Jeremy,' he continued, 'and there you will go. Think clearly.'

Jeremy shut his eyes, thinking of his father and Gillimal in the land of the giants and in a flash, the wizard was standing alone, as Jeremy and the horse travelled, invisible in the sky, towards the place Jeremy still held firmly in his mind.

21

Farewell to Old Friends

Jeremy left his father kneeling by the water and talking with Magdela and decided that it was time he said his own goodbyes. Looking around him, he saw so many that he had met along his journey but not the one who had always been by his side. He searched through the crowds for Gillimal but could not see him. But something told him to look upwards and when he did, he saw the shape of his friend, dark against the mountainside, as he climbed towards a nearby forest. Jeremy set off and clambered after him, working hard to match Gillimal's pace. When he caught up, he found him standing on a ledge looking out over the land, the sun shining over the many creatures below dotting the ground.

'And so it ends,' the Asrah sighed. 'Peace has been restored and our land is safe again. It could not have been this way without you, Jeremy, and Eringuild will remember your name forever.'

Jeremy felt suddenly sad and lunging forward, hugged Gillimal around his leg.

'Oh, Gillimal!' he exclaimed. 'I don't want to say goodbye. You have been the best friend that I've ever had!'

'And you have been mine,' said Gillimal solemnly, and he looked down at his young friend, feeling for the first time in all the many years of his life, a sense of what it was to love, as a father would love his child. But Asrahs are warriors and would never say such things, so he merely thought it and said: 'We will only say farewell, my friend, for I would be very surprised if we never met again.'

'How can you know?' Jeremy asked, his eyes shedding tears.

'The centuries have taught me many things,' said Gillimal wisely, 'and you can trust in that.'

They headed back down the hill, side by side as they had been throughout their quest, and were greeted by the cheers and shouts of everyone around them. Jeremy smiled shyly, looking at the ground, although he had never been happier.

Henry emerged from the crowds and walked towards his son, smiling with pride.

'It is a wonderful thing you have done here, Jeremy, and you have saved me as well as Eringuild,' he said. 'I would never have got home without you, but I promise,' and he sank to his knees, 'I shall never leave you again.'

Jeremy hugged him tightly.

'Are you ready to go home, Daddy?' he whispered, and his father nodded in answer.

22

From One World Back to Another

'We must return to the place you first entered,' Gillimal explained. 'Do you remember where that was, Jeremy?'

'Yes,' he replied. 'It was in my dream. A sharp edge looking over the valley below.' And a picture instantly appeared in his mind.

Once the many goodbyes were all said, the three companions set off together and it was not many hours until they were standing at that exact spot. 'This is the gateway back into your own world,' said Gillimal, 'and is the way you will travel home. You must think of it with all your strength and then take a running leap over the ledge. You will pass through the tunnel between the worlds and soon be home again.'

Jeremy was not altogether keen on this idea but believed Gillimal was telling him the absolute truth.

'I will go first,' said Henry bravely, and turned to hug Gillimal and thank him. He then turned to Jeremy. 'See you very soon,' he said.

Jeremy smiled and watched as his father took a leap over the cliff and vanished into the air as he did so. He then turned to Gillimal and simply said, 'Goodbye,' and then smiled, as there was no more to be said.

Gillimal smiled back as Jeremy ran towards the cliff and then disappeared just like his father.

His last glimpse of that world was an image of Gillimal standing on the cliff edge, tall and strong with one hoof raised in goodbye.

Jeremy swirled through the darkness, until he landed with a thump on what seemed like wooden boards. He opened his eyes to see that he was in the doorway of the secret room; the white sheets were still hiding the furniture, although there were no more secrets to be found there now.

Hearing a groan by him, Jeremy looked down to see his father sprawled on the floor. Henry had not had such a good journey from Eringuild.

'My head,' he moaned. 'I had forgotten how much that journey can hurt!'

'We're home!' said Jeremy excitedly. 'Let's go and find Mummy!'

'Just what I was thinking!' said Henry, and he held out his hand to his son. Jeremy hesitated and shook his head slightly.

'You go, Daddy,' he said. 'I'll be down in a minute.'

Henry nodded and walked down the stairs towards the kitchen, where the clattering of pans could be heard. Jeremy waited until the sound of his footsteps had disappeared and then walked back into the secret room.

Who would have thought he could have had such an adventure? He walked over to the desk and looked out into the garden. His old swing was swaying in the light breeze and he remembered Gillimal's words and understood now more than ever the importance of believing in strange and wonderful things.

Jeremy Applegate had fallen headfirst into an adventure, becoming part of another world, and he was sure as sure could be that one day, he would join them again. Jeremy smiled to himself as he left the secret room and slowly closed the door behind him.

17438824R00071

Printed in Great Britain
by Amazon